This can't be happening, I think, as Tomper's arms close around me. *Tomper Sandel and me?*

I don't know who is the first to pull away, but we both bounce away like springs. His eyes look silver for a moment, by the moon. He is smiling.

"You're a good kisser," he says.

"My first time," I admit. A strand of my long inky hair flutters, batlike, into my face, and Tomper gently brushes it away.

"Beginner's luck, then," he says, grinning. Why did I tell him this was my first kiss? I'm such a nerd.

Then I remember to check my watch. It is almost midnight.

"Oh no, Tomper," I say. "I really have to go."

"You turn into a pumpkin at midnight or something?"

"No, my parents will kill me if I'm not home on time."

"Well, see you later, 'gator," he says, giving my hand a squeeze.

I'll never wash that hand, I think to myself. I never imagined I'd catch myself thinking something like that. I run across the clearing to the Blazer. Thank God Jessie is there, ready and waiting—and smiling, because she knows I am going to tell her all about it, every detail.

We board the chariot, and it takes us rambling down the road, seemingly right into the huge harvest moon.

Finding My Voice

MARIE G. LEE

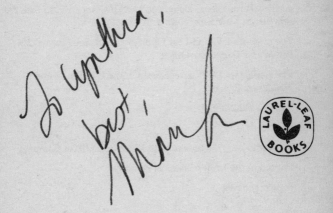

To Cynthia,
best,
[signature]

LAUREL-LEAF
BOOKS

Published by
Dell Publishing
a division of
Bantam Doubleday Dell Publishing Group, Inc.
1540 Broadway
New York, New York 10036

ISBN: 0-440-21896-9

RL: 5.3

Reprinted by arrangement with Houghton Mifflin Company

Printed in the United States of America

September 1994

10 9 8 7 6 5 4 3 2 1

✒ Acknowledgments

Many people have supported my effort to write this book, and I am sorry that I can thank but a few of them here.

First, I'd like to thank my family, who provided encouragement and love every step of the way. Thanks also to the Society of Children's Book Writers for their financial and professional support. I'd like to warmly thank writers Judy Blume, an eternal inspiration, and Nancy Willard, the world's greatest writing teacher, for all the help they've given me. Dear friends Carol De Matteo, Anne Fitzpatrick, and Tom French cannot go unmentioned here, nor can I forget the invaluable help from my agent, Wendy Schmalz, and my editor, Laura Hornik.

Lastly, all my thanks to Karl Jacoby, who not only read chapter one at least a bazillion times, but also has been there for me all these years with his intelligence, expert editorial advice, and dry wit.

To Mom and Papa

Finding My Voice

ℒ One

"MOOOO!" IT IS STILL dark when I reach to shut off the Holstein-shaped alarm clock that my best friend, Jessie, gave me for my sixteenth birthday. To shut it off, you have to pull down on the cow's enormous plastic udder. Mom wanted to throw it out. I told her it was just humor, Jessie-style.

I step into the steamy shower and let the warmth coax me awake. I shampoo, shave my legs, and let the conditioner sit in my hair for exactly five minutes, just as it says on the bottle. After toweling off, I put on deodorant, foot powder, perfume, and then begin applying wine-colored eyeliner under my lashes.

Do boys have to go through all this trouble day in and day out? How about Tomper Sandel, the football player who appears to be naturally cute with his shaggy blond hair and cleft chin — does he worry about how he smells?

I put on extra eye shadow in a semicircle around my top eyelid. According to *Glamour* magazine, this will give Oriental eyes a look of depth. I've always known that I don't have the neat crease at the top of my lid — like my friends do — that tells you exactly where the eye shadow should stop. So every day I have to paint in that crease, but I don't think I'm fooling anybody.

"Hurry up, Ellen," Mom calls from downstairs. I throw on my new Ocean Pacific T-shirt and jeans and run down.

Mom is standing in the kitchen, quietly spreading peanut butter on whole-wheat bread. She turns to look at me, and her eyebrows dip into a slight frown.

"Is that what you're wearing to school?"

"Yes, Mom," I say. We go through this scene every year.

"What about all those good clothes we bought in Minneapolis?"

"Those dresses are great," I say. "But no one wears a dress on the first day of school."

"Oh," Mom says, as if she's not convinced. She turns to finish packing my lunch. As usual, Father has already left for the hospital so he can get an early start on patients with morning-empty, surgery-ready stomachs.

I grab the Cheerios and milk, and eat while looking over my schedule one more time. This year, I won't have Jessie in a single class. She took typing and creative foods so that she can have more free time. In the meantime, I'll be sweating out calculus and trying to tack gymnastics onto my already-stuffed schedule. My parents say I have to take all the hard classes so I can get into Harvard like my sister, Michelle.

"Here's your lunch," Mom says, handing me a brown paper bag. I open it and find a small container filled with soft white ovals in sugary liquid.

"What is this?" I grimace, holding the tiny container aloft.

"Litchi nuts," Mom answers. "Remember? You love them."

"Not for lunch," I say, a little too vehemently. The truth is, I don't want people seeing those foreign-looking nuts and asking what they are.

Then I remember that every day Mom packs Father's lunch, then my lunch, while I'm up in the bathroom doing my deodorant-perfume-powder dance.

"Well, thanks, though, Mom," I say. "Could I please have a Hershey's bar from now on?"

Mom smiles. She is so thin and small in her gown and robe. I throw my lunch in my knapsack and kiss her quickly.

"Goodbye, Myong-Ok. It's your last year here," she says. I look up at her, upon hearing my Korean name. To me, it doesn't sound like my name, but to Mom, I think it means something special. Sometimes, I think she has so much more to say to me, but it gets lost, partly because of the gap separating Korean and English, and partly because of some other kind of gap that has always existed between me and my parents.

*

On the way to the bus stop, I slip the container of litchi nuts into a garbage can alongside the road. Wasteful, I know, but I'm always so nervous on the first day of school. All those kids. Especially the popular ones.

Everyone is at the bus stop — the same faces from last year, and the year before, and the year before that, but my throat still constricts. I wish Jessie lived nearby so she could take the bus with me. Two of the hockey players, Brad Whitlock and Mike Anderson, are loudly hooting and swaggering as if they own the place. I slip back and try to become invisible.

When the bus comes, student bodies swarm around the door like eager bees waiting to get into the hive. I let most of the kids go ahead of me, but as I board, someone shoves me from behind.

"Hey chink, move over."

In back of me is Brad Whitlock, a darkly adult look clouding his face. The sound of his words hangs for a moment in the cramped air of the school bus. Numbly, I look around. Everyone seems to be looking somewhere else: out the window, at their books, just away. Brad pushes past me to the back of the bus, where he resumes guffawing with his friends.

I sit gingerly in the nearest seat, like an old lady afraid of breaking something. I feel so ashamed, and I don't know why. And why Brad Whitlock, the popular guy who had never before even bothered to acknowledge my existence all these years at Arkin High? I keep my eyes fixed on the landscape and concentrate on keeping them dry.

As soon as the bus doors open at school, I rush out without looking back. Once I join the tide of people flowing into the brick building, my heartbeat finally starts to settle. Now I feel protected, anonymous. Inside, excited voices unite in a single deafening roar, punctuated by the staccato of slamming locker doors.

"Hey, Ellen!" Jessie's voice rises above the din. She will never know how glad I am to see her familiar face.

"Hi, Jess!" I say, keeping a falsetto of cheerfulness on my voice.

"Are you okay?" Jessie's big brown eyes study me closely. Then the prefinal bell rings.

"I'm fine, thanks, Jess." I slam our locker door, imagining that Brad Whitlock's fingers are caught in it.

Maybe someday I'll stop to really think about it, about what it means to be different.

*

The prefinal bell means that I have one minute to get to room 2-D, the chemistry classroom. I see my friend Beth sitting in the corner by the window. I also see Tomper Sandel — all muscles under his Arkin High Football T-shirt — sitting in the same row.

Crossing the room to join Beth, I pass Tomper's desk.

"Hi, Ellen," he says, and smiles.

"Uh, hi Tomper," I say, trying not to stare. Tomper Sandel — saying hi to me?

"Ahem," says Mr. Borglund, our teacher, as he stands in front of the class. He looks like a cartoon character: his skin is as dark and wrinkled as a dried apple, and his hair — which I'm sure was blond in his younger years — stands straight and stiff, the color of a Brillo Pad, on top of his head.

When he tells us to pick lab partners, Beth and I quickly choose each other. Mr. Borglund ushers us all across the hall to the lab room, which has rows of black counters with sinks and weird spigots crusted with powdery precipitates of experiments past.

"Chemistry is based on the metric system," Mr. Borglund says to us. "For instance, instead of pounds, we have grams. There are 454 grams to a pound. Familiarize your-selves with the meter sticks, scales, and graduates in your lab kits. Then do the problems I'm handing out."

Beth and I dig out the tangled mess of beakers, scales, and rulers from our lab cubby. Beth starts balancing her plastic bracelet against the tiny gram weights, which look like metal Monopoly pieces.

"How was your summer?" she asks.

"Pretty good," I say. "Are you going out for gymnastics again?"

"For sure," she says. "You are, aren't you?"

"I'm planning on it," I say, thinking how Mom and Father had cautioned me that if any of my grades fell lower than an A, there would be no more gymnastics.

Mr. Borglund has given us three problems on converting from the U.S. to the metric system. It's almost too easy: once you know the formula, it's the same for all three. Beth works it out on her calculator, and I double-check the numbers to make sure they are absolutely right. Then I hand in the paper, after writing ELLEN SUNG and BETH ZEIGLER neatly at the top. We are the first group to finish. The two guys sharing our counter are fencing with their meter sticks.

We are putting the equipment away when Tomper pokes his head into our lab space.

"How's it going over here?" he asks. I look at him warily, but thrill at his faint smell of smoke; it reminds me of log cabins and chopping wood.

"We're just finishing up," Beth chirps. I give Beth a look to let her know that we'd better not give him any answers, since that's what he's probably here for.

"How's gymnastics going, Ellen?" He turns to me and grins, his chin folding into a perfect dimple — adorable.

"Our first meet is in a few weeks," I say, then add, "Beth is going out for it again, too."

"I'll be there," he says, giving the thumbs-up sign and smiling right into my face.

He walks away, hands casually thrust into the pockets of his faded Levi's. From the back, his gold hair curls down his tanned neck. What luck to finally have him in a class.

"He's gorgeous." Beth sighs.

"Too flirtatious," I say as coolly as I can.

*

English composition is the last class of the day. My interest perks up when I see Tomper Sandel walk in the door ahead of me.

I take a seat next to Beth, and we look up expectantly at our new teacher, Mrs. Klatsen. This class is one of those silly ones that they make all the seniors take to make sure everyone can read and write when they leave Arkin High. At least I've heard that Mrs. K. is supposed to be a good teacher.

Neatly stacked in front of her are *The Red Pony*, *The Good Earth*, *Tess of the d'Urbervilles*, and *The Complete Shakespeare*.

"Good books like these can open up worlds," she says, standing up regally. She must be at least six feet tall.

"Why not wait until the movie comes out?" calls Mike Anderson from the back of the room.

I look up at Mrs. K. She is smiling.

"Movies and TV are definitely entertaining," she says, not missing a beat. "But did you ever stop to think about how one-track they are? Movies and TV give you an entire picture and tell you exactly how to feel — they have the scary music and the canned laughter to make sure you get it right. But books, on the other hand, give you only the words; you have to use your imagination for the rest. It's more than entertainment: your imagination will help you get things from books that you'll carry with you for the rest of your life."

I look at Mike; his mouth is closed.

"For today, I'd like to see how well your vocabularies have held up over the summer. Pick your partner by writing down your first and second choice on a piece of paper."

How democratic, I think as I join the scribbling and scrabbling of pens. I write down BETH ZEIGLER, and then, as an afterthought, I put TOM SANDEL under her name. I tear the page out of my spiral-bound notebook and make sure it is folded up before I send it forward.

Mrs. K. sorts through the ragged papers and comes up with a list. Then she calls me to her desk.

"Ellen." Her eyes smile through her huge plastic glasses that make her look appealingly bookish. "Your last year's teacher, Mrs. Jaynes, told me about what a wonderful English student you are."

I try to smile modestly. It's true that English has always been one of my favorite classes.

"And a lot of people put you down for first choice."

Everyone knows I'm good with vocab words. I sigh to myself. *It's not like I'm popular or anything.*

"Whom did Beth put down?" I ask.

"Well, I thought that instead of Beth, I'd like to pair you with someone who needs a little help, and I wanted to make sure it was okay with you."

"Sure," I say hopefully. Maybe it'll be Tomper.

"I think," she says, "that Mike Anderson could benefit greatly from working with you."

I immediately think of Mike guffawing with Brad Whitlock at the bus stop this morning. Then Mrs. K. smiles such a straightforward, honest smile that I can't say anything. I like her too much.

So, Mike Anderson, the star hockey player with less-than-stellar brains, slides his desk along the floor like a scooter — until it bumps into mine.

"Hey, Ellen, how's life?" He grins suavely.

I pull out the vocab list, and his grin dissolves. "Ready?" I ask.

He rests his head on the desk and mumbles into his elbow, "Yeah."

The first word is *omniscient*.

"How about if we say 'God is considered to be omniscient'?"

"Yeah, sure," comes the muffled reply.

"Omniscient means all-knowing," I tell him for his benefit.

I do the next few words without seeing any signs of life from Mike.

"Here, you do the next one." I poke the pen into his hand, and he clambers out of his stupor with gruff surprise.

The word is *sentimental*.

He scratches his head for a moment, looks at the word, then looks at me. He seems so uncertain that I feel sorry for him. Don't they ever use *sentimental* in *Sports Illustrated*?

"Uh, how about 'They took a sentimental journey to the center of the earth'?" He beams. "Howzat?"

He might be popular, I'm thinking, *but he's sure not much to look at in the I.Q. department.*

Of course, when it is time to read the results out loud, we are called on for *sentimental.*

"It's your word," I murmur, giving him a nudge.

"Uh, sentimental. 'They took a sentimental journey to the center of the earth.' "

A pause. Then the class hoots with laughter. Even Mrs. Klatsen chuckles. Mike looks around and grins as if he planned to be funny.

That's what being popular is like — everyone thinks you're great no matter what you do.

"That's not quite it, Mike," she says. "Beth, you try."

"We became very sentimental when we heard our class song," she dutifully replies.

"Perfect," says Mrs. K.

I can't help wondering if Jessie's day is going any better. This is supposed to be our best year ever, she told me over the summer. A best year for best friends.

☙ TWO

IT IS DINNER TIME at the Sung household, and although she's absent, the presence of my sister still dominates.

"She was very disciplined," Father says as he begins slurping at his Korean soup. "Even when she was getting all A's she still studied hard because she knew that being at the top of her class in a public school like Arkin wouldn't guarantee her getting into Harvard."

I tense my back against my chair. What good will it do for everyone to keep parading all of Michelle's accomplishments in front of me? Today in calculus class, Mr. Carlson, the teacher, delightedly shambled over when he saw me. "How's Michelle doing?" was the first thing that popped out of his mouth. "Boy, she was a whiz at math," was the second. I sat there wondering if he knew what my name was.

I look down at my lasagna. Its tomatoey garlicky smell mingles with the smell of seaweed from Father's soup. Since Mom has always cooked something Korean for Father and something "American" for her, Michelle, and me, the smells are always clashing, usually ending up in weird, cloying odors.

"How was school today?" Mom asks.

"Okay. Not much new," I say, although there's so much I want to say, that I wish I could say, that I can't.

I mentally close my eyes and envision a different conversation.

"A boy called me a 'chink' on the bus today," I would say. Mom's mouth would open. Father's chopsticks would drop, sinking unnoticed into the murky depths of his soup.

"You poor thing," Mom would say. "What did you do?"

"I totally ignored him," I would answer confidently.

"How terrible to have to go through that," Father would say, and he'd take off his thick spectacles so that for once I could see the tenderness in his eyes.

"With all this stress I think Ellen should worry less about grades and more about having a fun senior year and making friends," Mom would add.

"I agree," Father would say, and he'd resume slurping down his soup. *Slurp, slurp.*

*

"Ellen, why are you staring at your food?" I look at Mom. Father is slurping away, his head close to the bowl, the chopsticks poling all sorts of seaweed and bits of fish into his mouth.

"Just spacing out, Mom," I say.

"Did you find out about the language department?" Father asks between slurps.

"Yes." I know I've told him this before. "The school has canceled classes starting this year because they can't get enough kids in it."

"Remember to make it clear on your school applications that you only had three years of French because of a fault of the school's, not your own," he says.

"Yes, Father." I stare at the curly lasagna noodles again. College applications have been slowly advancing, like a storm gathering speed. What's going to happen to me? Michelle was a genius, a high school hermit who studied her brains out. I don't even know if I want to go halfway across the country for college.

After dinner, I troop up to my room to study. I know most kids have to help with the dishes, and I do feel a little guilty leaving Mom with the crusty lasagna pan and the big pot of stuff that looks as though it's been scooped up from a pond — but Mom and Father insist that my studies come first.

As I spread out my books, I leave my Holstein clock prominently in view, so I'll know to call Jessie at 8:00, as I usually do.

✑ Three

"THERE'S GOING to be a keg party out at the Sand Pits on Friday night," Jessie says to me one day after school. We're Scotch-taping snippets of perfume ads clipped from *Seventeen* to the inside of our locker door: "Embracing makes things happen!" "Give the night to Tabu." "There's nothing between you and me except Sweet Honesty."

"Uh-huh," I say, nervously anticipating trying to wrangle Mom and Father's permission to stay out late. Obviously, I won't tell them I'm going to a keg party, but even getting permission to go to a movie can be a hassle.

"You know, we barely went out last year," Jessie says. "This is our year to have fun." She has been to a couple of the parties at the Sand Pits, which is an abandoned mine pit where the popular kids go practically every weekend in the fall.

"You're right, Jess, let's do it." I grab my calc and chemistry books from the top shelf and put them in my knapsack.

I'll leave the books lying conspicuously open someplace where Mom and Father are sure to see them.

*

"Hey, Ellen," Tomper says to me in chemistry on Friday, "are you going to be at the Pits tonight?" His strong forearms rest on our counter.

"Of course," I say, as if I do it all the time.

"It's going to be a good party — we're getting six kegs." His eyes look turquoise next to the black counter. A pack of Marlboros peeks, like an imp, from his shirt pocket.

Kegs. Beer. An illegal party. Mom and Father would kill me if I got caught. Not to mention that I'd get kicked off the gymnastics team.

Tomper sees me staring at his cigarettes. He looks down, then shoves the red and white pack all the way into his pocket, until the only evidence of it is the lump it makes.

"Thanks, Ellen," he says, grinning sheepishly. "I could really get into trouble with the football coach for these."

I squirm inside. I wish I didn't know he smoked.

"You know," I say tentatively, "it'd improve your running and endurance a lot if you didn't smoke."

Tomper looks at me, then fiddles with a beaker that I've just washed. "I'm trying to quit," he says, holding the beaker up to the light as if checking for spots. "At my house, cigarettes're treated like candy — and hell, things there are so crazy that you need to smoke two or three just to calm down. My brothers and me are always puffing away."

I shudder. Why don't his parents stop him?

"Hey, break it up over there." Mr. Borglund's voice

· 15 ·

booms. I immediately return to the lab equipment. I do not want to get on my teacher's bad side.

Tomper, however, heads back to his lab station at a pace rivaling Marcel Marceau's "Walking against the Wind." He stops to turn around and wink.

"Hope I see you at the Pits," he says.

*

"I'd like to go out with Jessie to the late late show," I tell Mom casually as I dry the dinner dishes.

Mom raises an eyebrow.

"Do you have all your homework done?"

My stomach is shrinking to the size of a prune.

"Yes — all of it." I am so glad Father is on call, because of the two, usually Mom is more sympathetic.

"Please — I'd really like to go."

"You'll come home right after the movie?"

Mom's face is soft in the kitchen light. It's hard not being like Michelle and staying in to study all the time. I want to please Mom and Father, but I also can't imagine being a senior and not going to at least one party.

"Yes, Mom," I say, but I'm suddenly thinking about what will happen to me if I don't get into Harvard, not because I'm going to a party, but because I'm not smart enough. I know for a fact that I'm not as smart as Michelle — just talking to her always confuses me; she uses such big, obscure words. I wish Mom and Father would give me alternatives. Instead, I feel I have to get into Harvard or fall into a black hole. Some choice.

Still, at 8:00, I back out our Chevy Blazer from the garage and drive across town to Jessie's.

When I pull up, her house is dark; her father doesn't

come home from the mines until late in the evening, so she doesn't leave the lights on.

I've never met Jessie's mom. One Thanksgiving, long before Jessie and I became friends, an Arkin High student killed her when he came barreling down the wrong side of the street in his pickup — apparently he'd been drinking while watching the football game.

I stare out at the night. I won't drive drunk tonight — or any night. No way.

Jessie opens the door to the car. "Hi, Ellen," she says. As she hoists herself into the Blazer, the flowery smell of Sweet Honesty fills the car, followed by a slight trace of cooking smell — fried something.

"Do you know how to get there?" I ask.

"Yeah, go down that dirt road behind the old Saint Andrews School, and I'll show you. It's a bit of a drive."

I have visions of taking a wrong turn and pitching the Blazer headlong over a cliff. But then I think of Tomper Sandel and the way he was talking to me in chemistry. I shift the car into gear.

"Okay, Jess, you're the navigator."

As it turns out, the sign to Karl Pit, a.k.a. the Sand Pits, is well marked. I even see a few cars driving into it.

"Duck," Jessie says as overhanging branches slap the windshield. I downshift and let the car bounce in and out of the ruts in the road. Our headlights bash holes into the peaceful darkness.

As the car pulls into a clearing, I feel as if we're at the county fair, with all the lights around: from the moon, car headlights, and the huge bonfire spewing sparks into the sky.

Shadowy forms move restlessly; laughter pops and crackles out of the fire.

A jean-jacketed blob immediately approaches us in the dark. The blob is Rocky Jukich, one of the "burnout" guys in our class. If you sit around smoking on the school lawn, as I've seen Rocky do, you're considered a burnout; and there has always seemed to be some kind of correlation between burnouts and trouble: smoking, bad grades, drugs, you name it. Right now, the red end of Rocky's cigarette looks like a glowworm in the dark. I can't tell where his mouth is.

"It's a two-dollar contribution tonight," he drawls.

Jessie and I dig awkwardly in the pockets of our tight Levi's and extract dollars.

"Have a good time, girls." He hands us two flimsy plastic cups.

"I'm sure we will," Jessie calls gaily as she pushes me toward a thick of kids where, I guess, the kegs must be.

"Ugh," she says, as we fall into a sea of kids shoving to fill cups. "Where's the line?"

"Hey, move it, you assholes!" Tomper bursts through an opening on the other side of the crowd. A keg is firmly attached to both arms. He is in a white T-shirt, no jacket, and his biceps dance as he heaves the keg to the ground.

"You guys want to break your legs or something?" he bellows to the kids standing around the kegs. "Get out of the way when someone comes through carrying a keg, for Christ's sake."

I watch with fascination as Tomper pierces the dull silver keg with the tap and starts the beer running. I hope he won't see me trying to pour myself a beer — I have no idea how a tap works. It just seems to be a long skinny hose with some small contraption at the end, not one of those huge levers with beer logos like the ones I've seen on *Cheers*.

"Well hello there," he says, his eyes suddenly finding me. "You made it."

"Yeah," I say, feeling my blood pressure rise.

"Here, give me your cup."

Tomper's strong fingers take my cup away. He presses the little contraption and beer fizzes out — first a golden foam, which he throws away, and then real beer. He politely hands my cup to me. His eyes are navy blue in the dark.

"Here, gimme your glass," he says to Jessie, who is standing open-mouthed.

When Jessie has her beer, Tomper gives me a wave and a smile as he walks away. I'm so surprised, I almost forget to smile back.

"Wow," Jessie says as we move toward the fire. "I didn't know you knew Tomper Sandel."

I take a swig of beer and am surprised by its cool, acrid taste. I am tempted to act as though Tomper and I have been buddies for a long time.

"Actually, Jess, he's just started talking to me in chemistry and stuff," I say, as we reach the fire. I am feeling better now that I see there's no sign of the police, undercover teachers, or my gymnastics coach.

"He's definitely on my Gorgeous Burnout List," she says, closing her eyes and letting the fire shine on her face. "Right up there with Rocky Jukich."

"Do you think Tomper's a burnout?" I ask. "After all, he plays football and hockey." Most of the burnouts like

Rocky abhor sports, and while I know that Tomper does smoke, he doesn't seem to get into the heavy trouble — drugs, skipping classes, fighting — that people like Rocky do.

"Sure, they're both from Rainy Lake," she says, speaking of the wooded part of town just outside Arkin that people always seem to be talking about in hushed tones. Apparently, there are some bad biker bars out there, and a man was rumored to have been killed at one.

"Oh," I say. No matter, anyway. Tomper is way out of my league.

Jessie and I notice Mike Anderson and some other hockey players tromping drunkenly out of the tall brush, dragging wooden railroad ties. They grab the ties like battering rams and push them through a narrow opening in the crowd of kids. The ties crash into the fire with a flurry of sparks, and Mike haw-haws like a moose.

"Some party, huh?" Jessie says to me.

"Hey, whash up?" Shari, one of Jessie's friends from typing, swoops into our personal space. Her pale hair has been permed and bleached so much that it looks like electrical wiring, and the last button she's unbuttoned on her shirt looks just a little too low.

"Not much," Jessie says, looking back into the fire. "Hey, what's the deal with the V-8s?"

My head swivels and I see that Marsha Randall and some of the other popular girls are sporting cans of V-8 — the vegetable drink — as if this is a health-food convention. Marsha is flirting with some football players, trying to step on their toes and giggling.

"Oh, those assholes." Shari takes a shaky puff from her Marlboro. I try to lean out of the way when the used smoke comes charging out of her nostrils. "They say they can't drink 'cause of cheerleading."

And gymnastics, I think to myself. Marsha is the captain of the team.

"What a bunch of showoffs, those cheerleaders," Jessie says, loud enough that Marsha and her friends can probably hear. I admire how Jessie says exactly what's on her mind.

In fact, the first time I met her, we were at a music recital, and she came right over and said she'd like to sit with me. I was surprised and flattered — I had no idea she even knew who I was.

She said she was going to play the *Moonlight Sonata.* Then she showed me her hands: she'd put on at least two cheap plastic rings — the kind you get out of gumball machines — on each finger.

"I wanted to get into the mood by wearing my Liberace look," she said, while I tried not to laugh out loud. I thought she'd take them off before going on stage. Instead, she waved her hands around before she sat down. I thought old Mrs. Matheny, our piano teacher, would have a heart attack, but she just sat there and smiled. Then Jessie played the most beautiful *Moonlight Sonata* I'd ever heard — the music was so pure that it drew tears to my eyes. I couldn't believe the sound was coming from Jessie, her big body crouched down to the piano, all those crazy rings moving to the music.

"It was the rings," she told me modestly, later. "You

want to come over to my house? Ever drink coffee before? It's good if you put a lot of milk and sugar in it."

Ever since, we have been inseparable.

If the cheerleaders hear Jessie, however, they don't show it. They keep giggling and talking to all the popular guys. Shari talks to Jessie about typing class. I mostly sit back and watch.

"Who needs another beer?" Jessie holds up her empty cup.

"I'll come with you," I say, even though I'm done drinking for the night. At the kegs, a white jean-jacket sleeve brushes mine, and I catch a whiff of a nice, sophisticated-smelling perfume. I look up to see Marsha Randall making, I guess, a V-8 and beer cocktail.

Marsha glances over at me just as I realize that I am staring. I start to smile hello — as I try to do every day in gymnastics — but I stop when I see that she's turning her back on me, as if I'm a little ant that she's seen but not noticed.

Jessie fills her cup and then sneers, once Marsha vanishes into the crowd. "So much for not drinking," she says. "Give me an *H-Y-P-O-C-R-I-T-E*. Rah rah."

"She's so pretty, though," I say wistfully.

"She's a real doorknob, you know," Jessie says. "I had her in Math One, and she could not figure out how to divide fractions for the life of her. She just sat around giggling. Finally, she got Mike Anderson to do her problems for her."

"I'm surprised he knew how to," I say.

Out of nowhere, I feel a touch on my back. Uh oh.

"Hey, Ellen." Tomper's voice.

"Hi, Tomper," I say. Now my back is burning.

"I'm going to get another beer," Jessie says quickly, and she scoots away.

"How do you like the party?" he asks, as the butterflies in my stomach start doing violent flip-flops. Tomper is standing before me, his biceps now hidden inside his jean jacket, which is frayed at the elbows.

"It's okay," I say, as my mind races for something clever to say.

"A great night for it," he says, as we start wandering away from the fire into the dark brush.

"You can see all the constellations from here," Tomper goes on, looking up at the sky of obsidian and ice. The heavy metal music from the party faintly bleeds into the night.

Then, like in a dream, I feel one of his hands close around mine. My heart beats like a tom-tom.

"There's the North Star," he says, pointing with his other hand. "You can find it by tracing the path from the Big Dipper. It comes in handy if you need to find your way home."

I look at Tomper in fascination. He looks like an angel, his gold hair a halo in the moonlight. A warm breeze touches my neck and gives me the shivers.

"If I followed the North Star," I say softly, "I think I'd just end up at the North Pole, not home."

Tomper's laugh covers me, mixing in with the sound of the wind disturbing the tall pine branches.

His head moves, eclipsing the moon. The next thing I

know, his mouth is gently pressing on mine. *This can't be happening,* I think, as Tomper's arms close around me. *Tomper Sandel and me?*

I don't know who is the first to pull away, but we both bounce away like springs. His eyes look silver for a moment, by the moon. He is smiling.

"You're a good kisser," he says.

"My first time," I admit. A strand of my long inky hair flutters, batlike, into my face, and Tomper gently brushes it away.

"Beginner's luck, then," he says, grinning. Why did I tell him this was my first kiss? I'm such a nerd.

Then I remember to check my watch. It is almost midnight.

"Oh no, Tomper," I say. "I really have to go."

"You turn into a pumpkin at midnight or something?"

"No, my parents will kill me if I'm not home on time."

"Well, see you later, 'gator," he says, giving my hand a squeeze.

I'll never wash that hand, I think to myself. I never imagined I'd catch myself thinking something like that. I run across the clearing to the Blazer. Thank God Jessie is there, ready and waiting — and smiling, because she knows I am going to tell her all about it, every detail.

We board the chariot, and it takes us rambling down the road, seemingly right into the huge harvest moon.

🖎 Four

THE FOLLOWING MONDAY, I arrive at school still tired out from all the excitement of the weekend. Jessie is already at our locker, and her eyes grow wide when she sees me.

"You know what?" she says in a low voice that makes my hair stand on end. "I heard Tomper Sandel talking about you this morning."

"About me?" I croak. That I'm loose? That he doesn't like me? That he likes me?

"Get this," Jessie says. "I was in the bathroom, and you know how you can hear stuff in the hall through the grates in the door? Well, I overheard Miss Priss-face Marsha Randall talking to Tomper, and I heard your name."

"My name?" I yelp. Is that good or bad?

"Yeah, Marsha said to Tomper, 'I heard you were with Ellen Sung on Friday night.'"

"How does she know?" I cut in.

"Maybe she saw you two together," Jessie says.

"What'd Tomper say?"

"He said, 'Yeah, I was.' Then Marsha said, 'Do you like her or something?' "

Or something. I visualize her delicate pink lips curling into a sneer. I'm just an insignificant gnat not worth Tomper's time.

"Then he said, 'If I do, Marsha, everyone will know in their own sweet time' — that sounds encouraging, don't you think?"

"I don't know," I say hopelessly. I think of inquisitive lips and hands touching in the night. Funny how life can swivel you around so dramatically from moment to moment. People in car crashes must feel like this: everything's fine one moment, then — crash!

*

I arrive at chem before Tomper, and I sit in the back of the room with Beth. He saunters in late and sits in one of the desks up-front. His golden hair lies in agitated waves, as if he's just been out in the wind.

Normally, I take assiduous notes, especially because this class is so important for a future pre-med student. But today, all I can do is stare at the back of Tomper's head and try to keep from sighing. There's plenty of feeling left from Friday night — enough to last a good part of the year. *What should I do with it if he doesn't like me? Maybe I should buy a pet.* I chuckle half out loud at this thought, and Beth shoots me a disapproving look. Mechanically, I finish copying down the carbon-atom roundup that Mr. Borglund is demonstrating on the board.

When the bell rings, Tomper evaporates. I rush out into

the hall, but then feel silly. Why, though, would he kiss me like that on Friday and not talk to me on Monday?

In English class, he is late again. He doesn't look at me when he goes to sit down. Beads of frustration form on my upper lip.

"Instead of the usual Monday grammar test, we'll do an exercise," Mrs. K. says. "I've taken these sentences out of *The Good Earth*. Make each underlined adjective into an adverb and put it in a sentence of your own, preferably one that has something to do with the story. We'll do this with partners. Just push your desk over to the person on your left."

The person on my left is Beth. When I look behind me, I see that the person on Tomper's left is Marsha Randall. They are already leaning over each other's desks and laughing.

Beth and I dutifully add an "ly" to all the words and make sentences with them. We're finished before everyone else, so Beth sits serenely, completing her homework while I sit and try not to think about what's going on behind me.

When the hour is finally over, I gather my stuff and march toward the door. Then, because I can't stand it any longer, I pretend to pick a piece of lint off my shoulder and look back.

Tomper and Marsha are still laughing away. In fact, their desks are still pushed together and their heads are close, his golden hair and her albino-white hair mixing, like the pile of gold the girl in the fairy tale spun from straw. I guess that makes me Rumpelstiltskin.

*

I love gymnastics because any hurts that I feel come right out when I leap through the air. I can stretch and stretch my muscles to the breaking point, until they hurt more than my feelings.

But today, in the locker room, I hear Marsha say to a friend that she has suddenly decided to "go for" Tomper. When I watch her during practice — her beautiful hair and long strong body — I can't see how Tomper could possibly like me if he can have *her*. Jubilantly, she does a row of perfect back handsprings and then a back somersault. She has three stars on her leotard because she's lettered every year. I don't have any stars on mine, but I'm working on it.

"Did you do the calc homework?" Beth's squirrely voice is behind me. Even her leotard has one star sewn on it.

"No," I say, sighing. "I guess I'll go home and do it now."

✍ Five

IT IS LAB DAY again in chem. Beth and I are hustling, bumping elbows because there is a lot to set up in this experiment. We are supposed to suspend a stoppered test tube over a Bunsen burner. I adjust the clamp on the test-tube holder and then concentrate on sticking the thin glass pipette through the hole in the rubber stopper. I must have pushed too hard because I hear a splintering crack from inside the stopper.

"Argh," I say, removing the pipette. Small shards of glass tinkle out.

"What's up, girls?" asks Mr. Borglund as he lumbers over to our lab station.

"I broke a pipette," I say. "I'll pay for it."

"Oh, you don't have to do that." He peers strangely at Beth and me through his Coke-bottle glasses.

"You Orientals are always trying to save money," he says, smiling a suddenly evil grin.

"Huh?" I say.

"Are you Chinese or Japanese?" he asks. I look at him.

Then I turn and see that Tomper has stopped what he's doing and is looking straight at me. Right into my eyes.

"Korean," I say softly.

"Oho, you Koreans!" Mr. Borglund rumbles like a thunderstorm gathering speed. A few curious heads pop up in the lab.

"You Koreans WOK your dogs!" He explodes into high-pitched giggles, his mirthful face inches from mine.

This can't be happening, I think to myself. I have a crazy urge to pull the chain of the emergency shower, so I can melt and flow down the drain.

Mr. Borglund walks away, still chuckling.

I blindly try to stab another pipette into the stopper. My stomach lurches, as though trying to get out of my body.

"The burner's set up," Beth says without looking at me. We are moving gingerly now, avoiding elbow contact at all costs. I want to tell her that being Oriental isn't catching.

"Ellen," Tomper says. He is not grinning. His eyes are steel blue. Or is it steel gray? I bet my eyes are as flat as mud-colored disks. The way they always are. I turn my back on him, on the world, and I don't look up for the rest of the hour.

*

"Ellen, you've got to tell me what's wrong," Jessie says frantically. I am poised for a quick getaway: books, gymnastics stuff all packed and ready. But big blobs of tears ooze from my eyes.

"Here," she says, handing me a fluffy wad of tissues and taking my knapsack. "You're coming home with me."

At her house, Jessie lugs a two-gallon tub of vanilla ice

cream from the freezer. She nearly strains her back putting a scoop through it. Then she opens a can of cherry-pie filling and globs the viscous too-red stuff on top of the ice cream. With a sweep of her arm, she clears a bunch of gloves, hats, and records off the kitchen table, puts down the bowls, and hands me a spoon.

"Now that we are in the right environment," she says softly, "will you please tell me what's wrong?"

I dig into the ice cream. When the first cold spoonful enters my mouth, I find it strangely satisfying.

"You'll never guess what ha . . . happened, Jess," I say. A stray tear plops onto the sundae with a small splash.

"Tell me," she says.

"I broke a pipette in chemistry." I hiccup and shove another spoonful of sludge into my mouth. "Then Mr. Borglund came up to me and said I didn't have to pay for it; that he knew Orientals try to save money by doing stuff like 'wokking' their dogs."

"What!" Jessie yells, catapulting a piece of ice cream to the floor. She rips out a paper towel and starts hammering at the floor with her fist.

"I can't believe it," she snarls. "What a fucking asshole!"

My toes curl up in my socks. This is an adult we're talking about. The teacher. I look at my sundae, which is melting into abstract art.

"Did you tell the principal?"

"What?" I say. "Tell him what?"

"Tell him what Mr. Bigot Borglund said to you."

"Come on, Jess, he's the teacher," I say. "And what am I supposed to say, 'Mr. Borglund was telling jokes in class'?"

"That stuff isn't a joke," she fires back. "Why do you think it's okay because he's a teacher?"

Because I'm supposed to respect my elders, I am thinking. *Because I need an A in chemistry, and I'm too afraid to make waves.*

"I really think you should tell the principal," she says.

"I can't." The truth pops out, like a fish onto land. "I mean, what will it do? They won't fire him."

"He should know that it hurts you, that jerk. Plus, kids shouldn't have to listen to that stuff."

I think of Tomper. Then I think of Mom and Father. How would they react? I'm sure it wouldn't be good. Father would probably be worried that it'd somehow wreck my chances for Harvard.

"Do you want some coffee?" Jessie asks.

"Sure," I say.

Jessie throws two microwave coffee bags into the oven. When it dings, coffee aroma fills the tiny kitchen. I like the bitter jolt I get when I take the first sip.

"Has stuff like this happened before?" she asks, coffee steam curling gently around her nose.

There have been lots of times. They have fallen so far apart in the years of my life that I seem to be able to push away the hurt of one long before the next one happens.

"A few weeks ago," I tell her, "Brad Whitlock called me a 'chink' on the bus in front of all the other kids."

"Oh my God," Jessie says, putting down her coffee. "Did you say anything back to him?"

"No," I say weakly. "I sat down."

"Oh, Ellen," she says. "Why didn't you tell him off?"

"I don't know. I didn't know what to say."

"You should've said anything," she says. "Any four-letter word that came to mind. That scum deserves it."

"Oh, Jessie," I say, laughing for the first time today. "I wish you had been there."

"Me too," she says. "I'd have broken his eardrums. What an unbelievable jerk."

"But I *am* different, right?" I say.

"You're the same old Ellen," she says. "I've never thought of you as being different — in a bad way, that is. You are different because you're so smart."

"Why do you think people hate me?"

"They don't hate you," Jessie says. "They're jealous."

"But I'd never say mean things to Marsha Randall, even though I'm totally envious of her," I say.

"Exactly. You're not that type of rotten scummy person," Jessie says. "Besides, don't be envious of her. I smell a rat every time I smell that 'Les Temps de Paris.' " She says it like *Less Temps dee Pairiss*.

"Oh, is that what it is," I say. "I thought it smelled nice."

"She's a stinkweed," Jessie says. "You know, right after my mom died, it was training-bra time. Dear old Dad was cool enough to take me to Shrafft's, where we ran into Marsha and her Mom. I said hi to Marsha, and Dad tipped his fishing hat to both of them. And you know what? Marsha just looked at both of us like we were twin wads of gum she'd just discovered on her shoe — and she *knew* my mom had just died."

I swirl my mud-colored coffee round and round.

"I guess beautiful doesn't always mean great," I say, partly to myself and partly to Jessie.

"No way," Jessie says. "And you know what? I don't give two cents about what people think anymore. When you think about it, why should you care about an opinion from a jerk?"

"You're right," I say. But then I think of Marsha and her platinum tresses and her letter jacket with the gymnast on it. She can have all that and Tomper too, and she can shine and shine. No one knows she's nasty except Jessie and me and some other people at Arkin High who are too insignificant for her to bother with, anyway.

"So don't let the turkeys get you down," Jessie says to me as she clears the coffee cups. They've left rings all over the table, like crazy Olympic logos.

Six

I STUDY CHEMISTRY with a vengeance now. Mr. Borglund is his normal self: he doesn't give me any more or any less attention than he used to. I try glaring at him every so often, but it doesn't seem to register with him. Shouldn't he feel at least a little bad? Or did he tell the joke perhaps thinking I'd enjoy the special attention?

But even worse, Brad Whitlock has been chosen as a homecoming candidate, which confirms his popularity.

"I didn't vote for that dickhead," Jessie says. We're sitting on the school lawn, shivering a little in the autumn breeze and watching the colorful tempera-painted signs of people's names being hoisted up, one by one, onto the school's facade.

"I didn't either," I say. How is it possible that someone like Brad, who takes pleasure in humiliating someone else, can be so popular?

"Look," I say, poking Jessie in the side with my elbow. The name MARSHA RANDALL is going up.

"Figures." Jessie snorts. "The meek shall inherit the earth."

Sometimes I think things like homecoming are meant to tell the popular kids what they already know and make the rest of us feel like we've been left behind.

"Who'd you vote for?" I ask.

"Rocky Jukich, among others, naturally," she says. "Of course, I don't expect him to get elected."

The pep clubbers continue to attach the signs to the school's facade; I hope no one falls off those rickety ladders.

Then a sign catches my eye: TOM SANDEL. Tomper's name, in fire-engine red, is there for all to see. I voted for him even though he hasn't talked to me in a while.

"Tomper has been called up to greatness — it's nice having someone nice for a change," Jessie says. "I voted for him."

"Me too," I say, but I know I have no other claim on him except I know that our lips touched that silvery night in September. I lie down in the grass and look up at the sky.

"I think that cloud looks like Nancy Reagan," Jessie says, pointing to a fluffy cumulus cloud whose dark gray etching makes it look as if it has a prissy expression.

"I think you are a nut," I answer and sit up. They've just put up the last sign: MIKE ANDERSON.

"Sorry, Jess," I say. "No Rocky."

"Figures," she says, gathering her stuff for the next class. "Sometimes I don't know if this majority-voting stuff is such a great idea."

I think of all the people who voted for Brad Whitlock — maybe even some of the people who heard him call me a chink on the bus.

"You're right, Jess, it sure makes life shit for those of us stuck in the minority," I say, surprised that I used a swear word.

*

At gymnastics practice, all the girls crowd around Marsha Randall, the new homecoming celebrity.

"Congratulations, Marsha," I say on the way to my gym locker.

"Thanks, Ellen," she says, flashing me a Pepsodent smile. I pause for a moment and really try to like her, even if she is going to kill any chance I might have with Tomper. She is so beautiful with her hair spilling all over her shoulders.

I walk over to my locker.

"Hi, Beth," I say, covetously watching her hang up her flashy emerald green letter jacket.

"Set for the meet tomorrow?" Beth takes off her blouse, revealing a breadboard chest and scrawny arms. How she has all that power to pull and catch herself on the bars I'll never know.

"I guess so," I say, opening my locker. The dank odor of someone else's sweat socks, rust, and sickeningly sweet talcum powder assaults my nose.

"They really need to put in more lockers," Beth says, shoving her enormous pile of books into hers. "I hate sharing with the basketball players."

Barbara, our coach, threads her way among all the adolescent bodies over to us.

"Uh, hi," I say, feeling stupid in my bra and panties. Instead of looking at her face, I look at her thickening waist.

"Ellen, you're going junior varsity floor and beam tomorrow," she says, tapping the roster with her pencil. I steal a look at her face. Her auburn hair is in one of those short page boys that look permanently curled under.

"O-kay," I say as cheerfully as I can. I can't understand why I am being put on JV as a senior. At the end of last year, I was competing in varsity meets.

"Ugh," I say, when Barbara is gone.

"That's unfair," Beth says. "You're doing really well."

"I guess I need to learn some harder moves." I sigh.

"It's only the first meet, anyway," Beth says encouragingly. "You'll get your letter this year for sure."

"I can only hope," I say.

*

Tomper is at the meet, as he promised me that day in chemistry — way back on the first day of school. He is up there in the bleachers with Mike Anderson and Brad Whitlock. Compared with Mike and Brad's short, neat haircuts, Tomper's bushy hair looks long and wild. But all of them are wearing their letter jackets with the big *A* on the front, and Tomper doesn't look like a burnout at all.

I really wish I were going on varsity today of all days.

"Hey, Ellen." Jessie appears on the gym floor with me. She is waving a cardboard sign around, but pretending that she doesn't know I can see it. It says GO L N.

"Good luck," she says. "Also, I think someone you like has skipped football practice to be here — and someone you don't like, too."

"I know," I say casually, although my pulse is jumping around like a crazy fish. If I screw up, I will look bad not only in front of Tomper, but Brad Whitlock too — and I don't want that to happen.

Our competition, the Aurora-Hoyt Lakes team, is so small that they have only three people on JV. Their team color is crimson, the same as Harvard's. This would have been a good meet for Mom and Father to see, but they never come to my meets. Michelle never did any sports — in fact, she loathed gym class — and she got into Harvard, so Mom and Father probably can't see how sports fit into the great Harvard Equation. A dummy variable, at best.

We settle ourselves in the sidelines to watch the Aurora team start the JV beam event. Marsha Randall and some of the other varsity girls are stretching and doing handstands as if there isn't a meet going on.

The first Aurora girl hops onto the beam like a creeping toad. Her short legs and long toes grip the beam for dear life.

"You should be able to clean up here," Beth whispers to me. The toadlike girl wobbles on her legs but doesn't fall off. I roll my eyes at Beth and wish, once again, that I were competing varsity.

"Good luck," Beth says when it's my turn. Her bony elbow hits my rib cage in encouragement. Barbara goes out to help me place the vault springboard by the beam. I pull down my leotard and take a deep breath. Then I raise my hand to signal the judges. From opposite corners, the two nod simultaneously.

The springboard thumps woodenly as I hit it. When I land on the beam, I realize I have the most wonderful view from up here. I can see the bleachers, the judges, the side-lines. Everyone. The only problem is that they're all staring at me.

I leap and dance my way down the beam — moves that I've practiced a million times on the chalk line drawn on my bedroom floor. My back feels nice and supple today, so it's easy for me to do the trick where I bend backward, grab the beam, and swing my body over. My bare feet hit the beam accurately with a quiet *slap-slap* on the wood, and I hear cheers from our side of the gym. I feel a smile tugging at my lips as I finish my routine and dismount.

I trot back to my waiting spot, and Beth pats me on the back with her taped fingers. From where she's sitting, Barbara calls, "Nice job, Ellen!"

The little kids who serve as runners lift their scorecards high: 7.10 and 7.15. A full point higher than anyone on Aurora's team, which means I've probably won the event. Another cheer rises. I look up in the stands and see Jessie. She is holding up the GO L N sign, which on the back reads 10.0. I can't see what Tomper is doing.

In the floor exercise, the Aurora JV team is much braver at tumbling than I. The toadlike girl throws wobbly back handsprings and a shaky back somersault, her head dipping dangerously close to the mat. When she waves to the judges after her routine, I notice that her back arches so much that it makes her stomach stick out — it reminds me of little kids in swimsuits. She can't be more than a freshman.

Hold your head up, I tell myself fiercely when it's my turn to go out. I nod to Barbara, who puts on the "Gymnastics

Rhythms" album, the one record we all pick songs from. My body automatically tenses upon hearing the linty crackle that precedes my routine's song.

"Ain't she sweet," giggles the piano. "Walking down the street . . ." Crackle.

I run, jump, and walk around like Charlie Chaplin. I do my showy moves, a no-hands cartwheel and a back handspring. I end the routine with a jump that you can do only if you're very small and flexible: I jump up waist-high and touch my fingertips to the toes of my outstretched legs. People cheer. I take second place to the toadlike girl.

When the JV meet is over, the varsity meet begins. By then, more people have come in, and the gym is quite full.

Marsha is as cool as a cucumber, swathed in her varsity sweats like on a fashion shoot for *Vogue*. She's one of the few people on our team who compete in all four events.

When it's her turn on the beam, I peek out to spy on Tomper to see how involved he looks. I can see only Jessie, who is absently fanning herself with the sign.

Marsha jumps up lightly as a cat and bends her body close to the beam. Then she literally dives backward, bringing her legs with her so that she reaches a perfect handstand, which she holds for the judges' inspection. The audience collectively sucks in its breath. Then she lets her feet land, one exactly behind the other.

"Wow," says Beth, over the cheers. "A Valdez."

Of course, Marsha wins the beam event.

"Good luck, Beth," I say, when her turn comes for the uneven bars. She pulls her leotard down a final time and scuffles over to the judges. When she gets there, she timidly waves to each judge, her hand barely making a motion from her limp wrist.

I love the Jekyll-and-Hyde change as Beth charges the bars, hitting the springboard with a *thunk* surprisingly loud for someone so small. This always astonishes the judges after Beth's mousy salute.

Beth said she became good at bars by swinging from old iron railings on her farm. I picture her swinging in the hayloft as she swoops down fearlessly from the top bar and then hits the lower bar square on her hips, folding her body in half and making the bar bend inward with the force. She pulls herself up to the top, swings down again, changes bars, and twists — mad-dog Beth. For her dismount, she propels herself off the lower bar, zings through the air, and lands, fighting for a second not to take a step, then doesn't. I clap wildly.

The big event, though, is Marsha Randall doing the floor exercise. The Aurora girls seem to apologetically rush through their floor routines so Marsha can go.

Even Marsha's song is a special one. It is a Spanish dance with full instrumentals, including maracas, played on a tape player hooked up to a sound system — no tinny pianos from "Gymnastics Rhythms."

At her cue, she runs full speed down the diagonal to do a series of handsprings and back somersaults, then melts into a dance, her long legs striding and her blond ponytail streaming out behind her like a kite's tail. She runs down the diagonal again, doing a no-handed cartwheel and then flipping into back handsprings. Marsha is the only one who's succeeded in sewing together beautiful dancing with a strong tumbling routine.

People stomp and cheer for Marsha, the star. She graciously gives us all her bright white smile, bows to the judges as though this is the Olympics, then trots off to the trenches, where Barbara is waiting with a towel and her sweats.

After the meet, Tomper climbs down from the bleachers.

Come talk to me, come talk to me, I chant mentally, as I stand in the middle of the gym waiting for Jessie.

"You did really good, Ellen," he says, grinning and walking over.

"Thanks," I say, feeling self-conscious of my skinny body in a tight green leotard. I must look like a grasshopper. "Thanks for coming."

"I told you I would," he says. "Remember?"

"Yes," I say. I look at him and imagine pine trees. I would give anything to feel his arms around me again.

"Tomper!" squeals Marsha, jumping into his arms, with her back to me. My stomach hardens when I see his arms close familiarly around her slim body.

I think of Tomper telling me about the Big Dipper and the North Star and finding my way home. I turn away to go find Jessie. She is over on the sidelines talking to Beth.

"You were really great," Jessie says, giving me a hug.

"That's right," Beth agrees. "Varsity material."

As we exit the gym, all three of us see Tomper holding hands with Marsha. Jessie grabs my arm to steer me out of the gym faster. I feel my heart croak a few times.

"I think I like him, Jessie, I really do," I whisper.

"It's not healthy for you," she hisses back. "Marsha Randall obviously already has her claws in him — it's not worth it."

I don't know what anything is worth anymore, I'm thinking as I pull my books out of my locker. Books, Tomper, letter jackets, parties, friends. Where do I fit into this mess?

🦎 Seven

"ELLEN SUNG HAS JUST set a new record for this class," Mrs. Klatsen tells us. I feel myself scrunching up in my chair because I'm sure everyone's looking at me.

"She's gotten a perfect score on the weekly vocab tests to date — six weeks! The last record was set three years ago at five weeks."

A polite round of applause rolls through the room. Beth grins at me excitedly.

"Hey, good job." Mike Anderson leans over to pat my shoulder. "I knew I picked a good vocab partner."

*

"Nice going, 'gator." Tomper catches up to me after class. We are in the middle of the hall, and I feel a small twinge of satisfaction when I see Marsha Randall pass us.

"Is that my new name? Gator?" I ask. Tomper is wearing a gray sweat shirt. No place to carry cigarettes.

"If you like it," he says. "It sticks. If your middle initial is an *E*, you can be El E. Gator. Get it?"

"Yeah," I say, thinking how my middle name is Joyce,

the name my mother chose for herself when she came to America. "It isn't, though."

"Oh well," he says, scuffing the toe of his sneaker on the dark stone floor.

Call me, I suggest mentally. *Say you'll call me.*

"I've got to go to practice," he says. As he walks away, he turns and grins, cornflake crinkles around his eyes. "And congrats again."

"Thanks again," I say. So much for mental telepathy.

*

"I broke a record in English today," I tell Mom and Father at dinner. Tonight, Mom and I get fish sticks and Father is having clear mung-bean noodles with his favorite five-alarm Korean pickles, the dreaded kimchi.

"What's that?" asks Mom.

"I got one hundred percent on our weekly vocab tests six weeks in a row — a new class record."

"Great," Mom says and claps her hands.

Father impales a piece of kimchi with his chopsticks.

"That's very good, Ellen," he says. "These grades are important because they'll still be counted in your applications to college."

He doesn't smile when he says this. He never smiles. The peppery, vinegary smell of the kimchi stings my nostrils.

"Michelle called today," Mom announces, dishing another fish stick onto my plate. "She was wondering when you want to arrange your overnight stay and interview at Harvard."

"I'm supposed to be doing that soon?" I choke on a non-existent bone.

"Myong-Ok, are you okay?" Mom leans over to look at me.

"Yes," I sputter. I am remembering how Michelle picked some schools out East that she wanted to see, visited them, applied, and then got into all of them — Harvard, Yale, MIT. It was easy for her.

"What schools are you interested in?" Father asks.

"Oh, I don't know. Probably Harvard, Yale, Carleton, Brown, Wellesley, Princeton, and Penn," I say. Over the summer, I had haphazardly sent for material from any school that looked even remotely interesting. Father looks at me as if I've lost my mind.

"I guess I need to do a little research," I say feebly. "But you know, Brown has a seven-year combined undergraduate/graduate med program."

"We'll let you see three schools, the way we did with Michelle," Father says. "But hopefully you'll get into Harvard."

"Three schools plus Harvard?" I ask.

"No," he says. "Harvard is one of them."

I sigh and mash up my fish sticks with my fork. Sometimes, I feel that Father has less of an idea of what's really out there in the world than, say, Mike Anderson does. Father seems to be living in a universe made up of only a few neat and orderly images: books, Harvard, good grades, being a doctor or a lawyer. I think of my head and its chaotic crush of ideas, worries, joys, and I wonder how I came to be so different from my father.

✐ Eight

AT GYMNASTICS PRACTICE, I watch Marsha as she executes some perfect back somersaults high into the air. She's been doing gymnastics since she was in kindergarten; I didn't join until ninth grade, and Mom and Father are still asking me at least once a week if it's taking too much time from my homework. If Mom had started me in kindergarten, I wonder if I'd be as good as Marsha is now.

Maybe I can learn something new and exciting on the beam. How about a Valdez, that great move Marsha did at the last meet? I can easily do one on the floor mat, so how tough can it be?

I see Barbara standing by the beam, so I approach her.

"I'd like to learn a Valdez on the beam," I say.

"Huh?" she says, looking at me as if I am growing a third eye. I know that Marsha is the only person on the team who does them, but why not me too?

I repeat myself.

"Can you do one on the floor?"

I walk over to the ratty green floor mat, sit down, flip over, and kick my legs to a handstand.

"Okay," she says. "Now try it on the line."

Barbara must be satisfied, because she has me climb on the low beam.

"Ready?" she asks.

I have to flip over and grab a piece of the beam that's behind me. If I miss, I could get my face smashed into the hard wood. Still, I say "ready" and push off.

"Oof," says Barbara as my flailing leg kicks her in the chin. I see the beam coming at my face, but her strong arms support me, and I have enough time to grab the beam.

"That's pretty good," she says. "Want to try again?"

"Sure," I say.

After practice, Beth and I take a few laps around the gym, and we then go to the locker room together.

"Wow," she says, taking out an economy-sized container of talcum powder. "I can't believe I saw you trying a Valdez on the beam. It looked really good." Clouds of scented white dust rise from her like smoke.

"With Barbara holding me up *and* on the low beam." I laugh, but my pride is tugging at the roots of my hair. I release my ponytail, and for a quick second, my reflection in the mirror lets me see that with my thick black hair and almond eyes, I could be considered almost pretty.

Marsha Randall and her friend Diane Johnson giggle and shimmy by us. Marsha looks at me. Her green eyes sparkle.

"Hey ching-ching-a-ling," she says as she passes. "Ah-so."

Diane Johnson looks back, then breaks into a fit of nervous giggles.

I feel as if I've been hit in the head with a brick. I turn my back on Marsha so she can't see my pride collapsing.

Expanding tears begin to blur my vision, and I bite my lip until I start to see spots in front of my eyes.

"Bye, Beth," I say, tilting my head back so the tears can fall back into my eyes. Beth stands there, dazed.

"Wait, Ellen," she says suddenly. Her bony hand grabs my arm. "I'll walk out with you." Beth throws on the rest of her clothes and slings her bag of books onto her shoulder like a shield. The only way out is to pass Marsha and Diane again. They keep preening by their lockers as though there's nothing going on, but I can feel the tension in the air.

"Ching chong Chinaman," Marsha says to me, as we pass.

"Shut up," Beth says, glaring at her.

"Hey, you shut up." Marsha's shell-pink lips curl back to reveal her Pepsodent-piranha teeth.

I am as dumb as a stone.

"Come on," Beth says to me. "Let's leave these imbeciles."

Marsha makes ching-chonging noises as we leave. I can hear them even when we're way down the hall.

"Fucking ah-so, who does she think she is?" The final echo reaches our ears.

"Are you all right?" Beth asks.

I feel a lump the size of a golf ball forming in my throat. Sticks and stones may break my bones, but why do these stupid names make me cry? I am a quiet person, I don't make waves. I like Marsha — why is she doing this?

"I think I want to go home," I manage to say.

"How're you getting home?" she asks.

"Walking," I say. "My parents went to Minneapolis for the weekend."

"At least let my mom give you a ride," she says, looking at me as if I might break apart and float away at any minute.

I nod. My stomach seems to have fallen into my shoes, and I feel physically sick.

*

At home, I lie on my bed, staring at the pictures of Mary Lou Retton and Nadia Comaneci that I'd cut out from *Gymnast* and *Life* magazine. A few tears squeeze their way out of my eyelids. I had been looking forward to going out tonight, but now I don't want to go out ever, knowing what Marsha Randall — and probably all those other girls — really think of me. I don't know how I can go back to gymnastics.

I wonder what Marsha is doing right now. Hanging out at the Pizza Palace? On a date with Tomper?

I guess I could use this time to study rather than mope. I have a sudden realization: I have never seen Marsha's name on the honor roll. I heard her tell someone once that she wanted to be a dental technician. Maybe when I get my M.D., I'll come back to Arkin to practice, and she'll end up working for me as a medical secretary. By then she'll have three kids with Brad Whitlock, and they'll both be fat. I'll end up firing her because I'll decide I want only people with college degrees.

I need to get away, that's it. Michelle, after all, skipped from Arkin to Cambridge and picked up new friends and even a Korean boyfriend without any stress.

"I was always mad that Mom and Father never sent us to prep school," she told me once, privately and bitterly over the phone. "The people in Arkin are so ignorant! Nobody respects intelligence; all they care about are parties, looking good, and having sex."

I've always wondered if she was called "chink" in high school, too, but I never got to know. Michelle always hoarded her emotions and snapped at anyone who came too close.

I spread the colorful catalogs on the floor, wishing I could just jump in and see all the colleges and all the people in them. Let's see, how far away can I get from Marsha Randall, Brad Whitlock, and Mr. Borglund? I scratch Carleton College, which is still in Minnesota, off the list. I grab the nearest catalog, *All About Brown*, and start reading.

By the time I go to bed, I have narrowed my choices down to three: Harvard, Brown, and Wellesley. Harvard is a given. Brown seems neat because, first, it doesn't have core course requirements, so maybe I'll have more room to choose a few English courses with all my science stuff, and second, its combined undergraduate/graduate medical program would be a nice way to take a year off my medical studies. Wellesley is a funny choice because I can't imagine going to a school of all girls, but it's the prospect of a total change that makes me interested.

*

At 5:30 in the morning, the mooing of a battery-operated cow is almost too much. I peer out the dark window. The trees in our yard are gray by the light of the street lamps, and everything is in suspended animation. I am awake ahead of everyone in Arkin.

Getting up early does wonders for me. In the quiet of the morning, I feel more alert, more creative, smarter.

I sit at my desk and open my calc book.

I am afraid of calculus, I have to admit. When I saw that Beth and I were the only girls in the class, I thought that guys must be naturally better in calc and that I had the right to be scared. But then I noticed that Beth was catching on to all the abstract calc concepts as soon as Mr. Carlson explained them, while I had to frantically copy everything down and later sit around for hours trying to decipher it.

All I know for sure is that calc is one of those classes that I need to get an A in to impress Harvard.

When I look up at the clock again, it reads 6:45. I get up and shake my legs.

The pewter morning light is just beginning to make its way through the windows as I head to the bathroom. On the way back, I stop in front of Father's study.

Father's study is the only room in the house that has a lock. I guess it's to keep out the kids, the mom. But I wonder what he does in there all the time, after dinner, on weekends. He doesn't need a lock just to read.

It's open now, so I walk in. I've never even gotten a good look into this room. Now I go into the center and take the time to stare and stare.

It is lined on two sides by rows of books that reach all the way to the ceiling. One wall is filled with oak-framed medical certificates. Father's black desk sits, like an island, in the middle of the room.

I sit behind the desk. His chair fits me pretty well because while I'm small, Father is extremely short — the top of his head comes up to Jessie's dad's shoulder.

I open one of the side drawers of the desk. Neatly stacked inside are several cellophane packages of those jellied Chuckles candies. Now why would he be eating Chuckles candy? I know that sometimes he likes to sample "American" things, but when he does, he takes exactly one bite, one package, or whatever, because by and large he finds American food very weird.

I really should leave, now, and let this be it. But some inner curiosity gnaws at my empty stomach. What *is* the story, I want to know. For instance, why are we in Arkin, Minnesota, of all places? When Michelle and I used to ask, Father would say nothing more than "because there was work here." He would never tell us what life was like in Korea or why he and Mom left. From what I've learned in my history classes, emigrating from a country like Korea wasn't as simple as deciding to go, packing your bags, and making the reservations on the boat. Did they go through Ellis Island and wave hello to the Statue of Liberty? I want to know all that. I want to know why I'm not like Jessie or Beth or Marsha Randall.

"Maybe they'll tell us something when we're older," Michelle had said after one of those times when we begged Mom and Father to tell us stories about Korea. "If there's some reason they don't want to tell us, I'll respect it."

I've always been the bad daughter, I guess. "Forgive me," I say out loud to the ghosts of Father's ancestors, in case they are watching.

In the small file cabinet near his desk, I find a file labeled "Michelle," and I pull it out. Inside are a bunch of report cards (all A's), a picture of Michelle receiving a national math prize, and acceptance letters from MIT and Yale. In a separate folder in the file lies the crisp parchment of her Harvard acceptance certificate. "We are proud to announce that MICHELLE SUNG has been accepted to the Class of . . ." Imagine, Harvard people think their school is so great that they feel you deserve a certificate just for getting in. I'm surprised it's sitting in here and is not displayed on the wall — or in a museum.

Of course, next to Michelle's file is mine. I'm not even sure I want to look. It's about as thick as hers, but I can't imagine what could be in it. I pull it out and start digging through it.

The same report cards, but with a few B's in math contaminating them, a picture from the *Tribune* of me with the gymnastics team — I had no idea Father even noticed that in the paper — and college catalogs from Harvard, Yale, Princeton, and MIT. Now why would *he* be sending away for this college stuff when it's supposedly me who's deciding where I'm going to school? And MIT? Doesn't he know his own daughter well enough to know that she hates math? What would he say if I went to a small school like Carleton or didn't go at all? Jessie doesn't think she's going to college, and she doesn't seem too worried about it. I cram the folder back into its place.

I then slide out the skinny middle drawer of the desk; I've saved it for last because I always keep my important things in there, and I thought Father might too. Inside are more paper clips, a letter opener, and a few silver dollars.

There has to be more. Why else would he have a lock on

the door? Sniffing like a pack rat, I start to paw around, looking in all the unlikely places I can think of: behind books, under the desk, even behind the medical certificates.

For some reason, I burrow behind his stack of classical records. At first, my hand passes through a gossamer cloud of cobwebs. Then it touches something flat and smooth — a book cover, perhaps. I stick my arm in farther to see if I can get a grip on it.

I pull out two thin scrapbooks, one on top of the other. Underneath the coating of dust, the leather covers are embossed with gold leaf.

I creak open the top one. The first page has a black-and-white photo neatly attached to the yellowing paper with small paste-on photo corners. It's of a bunch of doctors and nurses standing on the steps of a hospital, Santa Rosa Hospital, according to the sign. As I look more closely, I spot Father right away: he's the shortest and the only Oriental person. If I take him out of the picture, this could be a snapshot of a sitcom called *Surfing Doctors*, or something like that. Everyone looks so carefree, and those scrub suits could be surfer jams and the women in the cat-eyed glasses could be the bopping girlfriends in bikinis. Then there's Father, off to the side in his spectacles and his somber look, as if he's on the wrong set.

I remember Father mentioning that he briefly interned at a hospital in southern California. This must be the one.

When I turn to the next page, a folded newspaper clipping slips out. I have to keep my fingers as light as feathers to unfold the sepia-toned paper without ripping it to shreds.

"YOUNG KOREAN ÉMIGRÉ FINDS NEW LIFE IN THE U.S.," reads the headline.

"Dr. Victor Sung almost had his life ended in the war — before he ever set foot on American soil."

My eyes bulge as I read. This is Father? And what war?

"A young intern originally from Pyongyang, North Korea, Sung was hit by shrapnel from a bomb dropped near the barracks.

" 'Yes, I was very lucky,' said Dr. Sung, displaying the cross-shaped scar on his forehead. According to the surgeon who operated on him, the wound would have killed Sung had it been even as little as half an inch deeper."

Shrapnel? Killed? Father never mentioned anything about being in a war. And I never noticed any war wounds, although his forehead is already a map of wrinkles and crevices.

As I read on, the article details how Father, and presumably Mom, emigrated to the U.S. and how Father landed an internship at Santa Rosa Hospital in California. The article goes on about Father's "outstanding" work in surgical research. Why did he give it up, I wonder, for some small-town practice?

I turn to the next page of the album and find a very worn picture that looks almost as if it has gone through the wash: it's been creased and wrinkled so many times that it feels soft, like cloth. It is of a pretty Korean woman in a striped gown — which I'm sure was all sorts of vivid colors — holding a moon-faced boy, and there are a few solemn-looking men, also in costume, with funny T-shaped hats, in the background. No one is smiling — Father's expression. Maybe these are Father's relatives.

Another picture is of Mom in her wedding gown. She looks so young! Like a schoolgirl in a simple white dress. Is it possible that she had a crush on Father the way I have a crush on Tomper? But Mom and Father are so reserved that I can't imagine it.

Caught in the binding of that page is a glossy square of paper about as big as my palm; it looks as if it's been stuck in the binding for I don't know how long. On one side, it's just a patch of pink. On the other side, it has a picture of a lady in an old-fashioned pointy bra; she is holding a pack of cigarettes, and the words "Smoke ——, it's nicer," rise in a bubble from her mouth. The scrap falls out of my hands, and for a minute I consider letting it remain on the floor, but I notice that it's torn out in a nice, neat square. I carefully tuck it back into place.

That's the first book.

I open the second one to find a cache of airmail letters, all in Korean, wedged inside the cover. I unfold the crisp aerograms and just stare at them. It's such a hex not knowing Korean — a whole part of me is not there.

I remember that when I was younger, I found some Korean children's books that had colorful pictures of butterflies and Korean kids in pigtails. The book was chock-full of Korean writing, so I copied some of the squashed-bug symbols and showed them to Mom. " 'I want to go home, I want to go home.' " She'd laughed, reading my handwriting. Excitedly, I copied more and more and kept bringing them to her. Finally, she said, "No, Ellen. English is your language." And she wouldn't tell me about the squashed-bug symbols anymore. I still took the books into the closet and read them by flashlight — staring and staring at the symbols until they burned themselves into my retina. But the meanings never came.

Light is now streaming through the windows in Father's study, and I feel exposed, like a criminal, a vampire. I carefully replace the albums where I found them, and walk out of the room backward, making sure that it looks the same as before I entered. It does.

Well, folks, I just took my sentimental journey to the center of the earth.

Nine

WHEN MOM AND FATHER come home Sunday night, I show them my list of chosen colleges. Father raises an eyebrow at Wellesley and says he's never heard of it.

"It's a women's college," I tell him. "It's part of the Seven Sisters, which is like the Ivy League."

"I know the Ivy League is good because Harvard is in it," Father says.

"And Brown," I add. Mom nods.

"I've heard that Princeton is good," Father says, and my mind immediately flashes back to the folder.

"I'm pretty happy with my choices," I say. Is this a test to see if I'd pick the same schools as Father?

"I think it's good that Ellen is picking different schools from Michelle," Mom says helpfully.

Father doesn't say anything.

The next morning, I am poised with my list of phone numbers for arranging my interviews and overnight stays at the three colleges. Father hovers nearby, telling me what to say.

"Thank you very much. Have a good day. Goodbye." It sounds suspiciously like Michelle's old script.

Once the dates are marked in red letters on the wall calendar in the kitchen, I run out the door to catch the bus.

Between classes, I slip into the principal's office to get my advance-absence pass that has to be signed by all my teachers.

In calculus, Mr. Carlson's beady eyes light up when I show him the pass.

"Are you going to look at MIT?"

"No," I say. I've been in his class for two months and I swear he still thinks I'm Michelle. Doesn't he notice that I have trouble catching on? Doesn't he notice that my test scores are not all A's? He keeps saying that when Michelle was here, he needed a grade higher than an A to give her — he can't possibly get the two of us mixed up!

Mr. Carlson signs the pass C^2 (Corey Carlson = C squared) and beams at me. I am relieved to take my seat.

"Guess what, class," Mr. Carlson says, still beaming. "Ellen Sung is going to be taking a little trip. Want to tell us where you're going, Ellen?"

I resist the urge to crouch down under my desk. "To look at colleges," I mumble.

"Where?" Mr. Carlson prompts.

"Harvard, Brown, and Wellesley," I say quickly. I am wondering what's going to happen in April. Is Mr. Carlson going to make me name all the places I didn't get in?

*

"Remember," Mom says to me on the plane to Boston, "these visits are also for you to decide if you like these schools."

"Thanks, Mom," I say, although I still don't feel that I have much choice in the whole process. I pull back a corner of the foil covering my dinner. Gray meat in beige gravy stares back at me.

Will I know anything for sure beside the fact that being on the East Coast will separate me from Marsha Randall — and Jessie? I cover the dinner again with a shroud of tinfoil.

Mom is poking at the gray meat under her foil.

"Is it okay if I start on the dessert?" I ask, eyeing the square of chocolate cake in its little plastic dish.

"I was just thinking the same thing," she says, digging into her cake. I dig into mine, and we laugh. I am relieved that Mom isn't using this time — as Father would — to coach me on interview techniques or something.

From Logan Airport, we rent a car and drive out to Wellesley, where we arrive at the Wellesley Inn. It is a quaint white wooden structure with a dark green roof and shutters. Inside, a beautiful crystal chandelier sparkles right over my head as we check in.

Arkin has two places for visitors. The Days Inn sits right off of Route 9, so fishermen coming north from Minneapolis can stop for the night on their way up to the Boundary Waters. The nicer hotel, the Lakeview, used to be a Best Western until Mike Anderson's father bought it, which might explain the odd choice of name for a building that looks out onto Main Street. The Lakeview has a pool, a bar, and a special room for wedding receptions. With its nubbly orange-ish carpets and striped wallpaper, however, it can't even begin to compete with the Wellesley Inn's white-washed elegance.

Tonight, as we get ready to snuggle into the cozy bed, which has wooden headboards that look like half of a wagon wheel, I lay out my clothes for tomorrow's inter-view: bra, slip, and one of the light wool dresses that Mom and I bought in Minneapolis.

*

The next day, Mom drops me off at the admissions office on her way to explore the town of Wellesley. I have my overnight bag and a manila folder with my report cards. I stare sadly at the back of the rental car as she drives off.

"Hello," says the lady at the desk. Her gray hair is pulled back into a bun, and there are huge liver-colored age spots on her hands.

"Hi, I'm Ellen Sung, and I'm here for my interview," I say, then clear my throat because my voice sounds as if it's rattling.

"Please have a seat," she says, pointing with her spotted hand.

I perch awkwardly on one of the hard, needlepoint chairs. This room is so feminine, I notice. It has puffy cur-tains, soft-colored rugs under dark wood coffee tables, and chairs that no one would want to sit on for more than fif-teen minutes. I want to check to see if the needlepoint gets worn by all the people sitting on it, but of course I don't.

"Ellen?"

I look up to see a lady in a business suit.

"Yes, I'm Ellen," I say, extending my hand.

"Hello, Ellen," she says, returning my grasp warmly. "I'm Margaret McGrath, your interviewer. Welcome."

She leads me into a room that has a huge wooden desk, lots of books, and portraits of women — who I assume are famous graduates — on the wall. She sits behind the desk and motions toward one of the smaller chairs facing her.

"You've come a long way from Minnesota," she says, folding her elbows on the desk and looking expectantly at me.

"Yes," I say, already resorting to one-word answers. Father said that was a no-no.

"It's worth the trip," I add.

"So, why are you interested in Wellesley?"

I cross my legs at the ankle — the way *Glamour* magazine says you're supposed to do in interviews — and I try to look thoughtful, not overwhelmed, which is how I really feel.

"I've been interested in Wellesley ever since I noticed I was one of two girls in my calculus class," I say, then pause to hear how it sounds.

"I started to think about what it would be like to go to a college where the women run things. At my high school, a premium is placed on being pretty, which leads girls to believe that that's all they need to succeed in life. The crowning achievement for a girl is to be homecoming queen or a cheerleader, which really involves being pretty and cheering the boys on."

As I sit back, I realize the truth of these words. But did I need to come all the way to Wellesley, Massachusetts, to find that out?

"Very interesting," Miss McGrath says as she takes a look at my report cards. She smiles.

"You look as though you'd be an excellent Wellesley candidate," she says. "Have you taken your SAT's yet?"

"No," I say, and groan inwardly. Another thing to add to my "To Worry About" pile. "I'm taking them in November."

"Where else are you applying?"

"Harvard and Brown," I say.

She looks at me the same way Barbara did that day I said I wanted to try a Valdez on the beam.

"No back-up schools?"

Am I supposed to be applying to more?

"Uh, no," I say. I hate feeling like I'm on a game show where I'm trying to guess what she wants to hear. One wrong answer and *BZZZ*. Rejection letter.

We talk a few minutes more, then Miss McGrath rises out of her chair. I get up, too, feeling discombobulated. Already, in my head, I am playing back everything I've said, wondering if I've said it right.

"I've had a very enjoyable time speaking with you," she says, slipping me a cream-colored card. "If you have any questions, please call. I'm sure that after talking to some of the students here, you'll find Wellesley is an ideal place for a bright young woman such as yourself."

I soak up this compliment like a parched patch of soil taking to a cloudburst. *Bright young woman.*

"Thank you," I say. "Thank you very much."

As we return to the waiting room, I see a red-headed girl waiting for me.

"Hi, I'm Caitlin," she says, and I wonder how to spell

that. She is dressed in a kilt, yellow sweater, green turtleneck, and a hairband covered in a fabric that matches the plaid skirt exactly.

"So, where are you from in Minnesota?" she asks, as we stroll across the manicured campus.

"Arkin," I say.

Caitlin gives me a blank look. "I've heard of Minneapolis — is that near it?"

"Arkin is on the other side of the state, to the north," I say, trying to think of anything that Arkin might be known for. I can't think of anything except the mines.

"It's sort of near Hibbing, where there's the world's largest open pit mine," I say.

"Oh," she says. A vague flash of recognition. "The Mesabi Range. I read about Hibbing in *The Sleeping Giant*."

"Right," I say.

Caitlin's dorm is painted a delicate lemon-yellow and has a charming porch. I can see myself here with my bio books on my lap, my feet propped up on the railing, and a big glass of lemonade in my hand. There are two girls lounging: one is reading *Crime and Punishment* and the other a psychology textbook. Both are wearing Wellesley sweat shirts.

Caitlin's room is on the second floor, and it has the same unmistakably feminine touch as the admissions office. Her wall is graced by a single framed print of a flower, and her cosmetics are neatly stacked on a lacquered tray on her dresser. While Caitlin is intently studying something in one of her class notebooks, I stride over to look at a gem-shaped bottle that's caught my eye. "Les Temps de Paris" is engraved on its gold cap. I take a sniff at the bottle and bring the essence of Marsha Randall into the room. I quickly plug it back up.

"I think I'm going to freshen up," I say.

When I return to the room, Caitlin is still looking at her notebook. By her bed, I notice, are *The Advanced Theory of Mathematics, Discrete Mathematics,* and *Programming with Pascal,* all neatly stacked.

I take off my woolen dress, which by now has become stifling in the cozy afternoon warmth of this small room. Caitlin closes the notebook with a sigh.

"What are you majoring in?" I ask.

"Applied math," she says, taking off her plaid headband and beginning to comb her hair with long, broad strokes. "Also known as Apple Math."

"That's great," I say. I admire anyone brave enough to pursue math.

I pull on my old favorites: a long-sleeved Sid the Killer T-shirt — a happy souvenir from the time Jessie and I went to see the concert in Duluth — and my trusty Levi's. Then I notice Caitlin is giving me a funny look.

"Who is Sid the Killer?" she asks, finally.

"Oh, he does that song, 'The Flies of Summer.' It starts out 'Flies are vicious . . .' " I stumble a little on the tune.

Caitlin's bronze eyebrows are knitted together in puzzlement.

"They might be just a regional band," I add.

At dinner, Sid the Killer is even more out of place. Most of the girls are in skirts, even the athletes — Caitlin tells me they are field hockey players.

Caitlin introduces me to everyone at our table. The rosy faces look fresh and sincere. They all want to know where

I'm from, so I tell them about open pit mines. No one has heard of Sid the Killer.

"I met a really nice guy from MIT last weekend at the Alpha Theta frat party," the girl to my left says to Caitlin.

Caitlin chews her cooked carrots with interest. "Is he cute?"

"Yeah," says the girl, absently picking apart a dinner roll but not eating any of it. "I think we are going on a date this weekend, and I invited him to our house party."

"We have a very social house," Caitlin tells me. "We throw a party every couple of weeks. A lot of nice guys come up from Harvard and MIT — even as far as Yale."

"Uh-huh," I say. So that's how they "provide a diverse social life," as quoted from the school catalog. The few party pictures I saw showed a bunch of girls in skirts smiling and talking to guys in preppy sweaters.

I wait for someone to start talking about classes, but no one does, and I'm too shy to bring up the subject. I'm a little disappointed, because I got the impression from all three school catalogs that people spent mealtimes discussing heavy intellectual stuff. Perhaps I need to go to an intellectual house, since this is the social one.

There is an Oriental girl sitting on the other side of the room, and I think about getting up and going over to talk to her. But I decide not to: she's sitting with a bunch of people, and besides, I would probably be annoyed if someone wanted to talk to me just because I am Oriental.

After dinner, Caitlin goes downstairs to study. I drag out my calc book, which I've been dutifully lugging around, then I decide to call Michelle.

"Hi, Michelle," I say. "It's your kid sister calling."

"Hi there," she says. "How are things going over there?"

"Weird," I admit.

"How so?" she asks cheerfully.

"It seems like a great idea — all the women learning together," I say. "So I sort of expected to get my consciousness raised by all the feminine energy, but no one's really talked about any intellectual stuff, at least during dinner."

"That's Wellesley for you," she says, breaking into peals of derisive laughter. If I decided to go here, I wonder, would she still laugh?

"I saw only one other Oriental girl in the dining place I was in," I say, to change the subject.

"The right word is 'Asian,' Ellen," she says. "And don't worry, there are plenty in all the New England schools; you won't feel left out the way you do in Arkin."

I'm about to tell her that I don't feel left out in Arkin, when she plows me over with more words.

"Ellen, I've got a positively monolithic orgo test to study for. Good luck on your interview tomorrow."

*

The next morning, Mom comes to pick me up. I look one more time at the carefully tended grounds and the brick-and-wood buildings. When I said goodbye to Caitlin, she said she hoped she'd see me at Wellesley next year, and she gave me her name in case I had any questions later. At least now I know how to spell *Caitlin*.

"How did you like it?" Mom asks when we're on the road to Cambridge.

"It was okay," I say. At this moment, my opinions are

just a jumble of unfinished projects. I try to tell Mom about the good interview, the skirts, my math-minded overnight guide, and Michelle's trademark any-school-that's-not-Harvard-is-second-rate snort.

"There were some things I liked and some I didn't, but I don't know what's Wellesley and what's college in general."

"That's why it's good to look at a couple of schools," Mom says, gliding in and out of the swarming traffic.

"How did you choose where you went to college?" I ask.

"I didn't go," she says simply. Her hands are firm on the steering wheel. One of the tendons in her knuckle moves rigidly under her skin, like a worm. "I met your father and we got married."

Like a clam, Mom closes herself to that subject. Her eyes are still serenely viewing the crazy conglomeration of cars.

I wonder if Jessie misses me.

We park and start making our way to the admissions office. Mom is going to visit Michelle while I'm having my interview, and then we're all going to have dinner together.

The admissions office is an imposing brick building on a tree-lined street. My heart keeps jumping into my throat, and I swallow hard to keep it down.

"Good luck," Mom says, giving my hand a squeeze.

I walk through the door into what looks like a cavern, New England style: high wooden ceilings with light fixtures gracefully arching down like stalactites.

"Hello," says the woman sitting at the desk. She looks very uncomfortable in her thick tweedy suit.

I tell her I'm here for my interview, and she rustles a list stacked with names. She turns one page, then flips to the next. My stomach turns cold. What if I've made the appointment on the wrong day? What if they forgot to schedule me? I need this interview!

"Ellen Sung," she mumbles, as if I'm an acquaintance she'd known long ago but can't quite place. "Ellen Sung. Oh, here you are. Two o'clock. Please have a seat."

I seat myself in one of the elegant armchairs. Across from me is a boy in a gray suit — not the slightly unmatched kind guys in Arkin get from the Casual Male, but a miniature of the one Father wears when he's dressing up. Gray Suit sizes me up with one sweep of his beady eyes and then probably decides I'm a Midwestern hick who wears Sid the Killer T-shirts.

I grab a copy of the *Crimson*, which appears to be the Harvard newspaper, and do my best to look nonchalant.

"Talbot Haverhill, Junior?" booms a voice from the hall.

"That's the Third," he says, as he gets up stiffly and marches like a robot toward the voice.

"Ellen Sung?" booms the same voice. It makes me feel that I need to pick up my little dog Toto before I follow Gray Suit down the hall.

"Hi, I'm Jeff Rose."

Jeff Rose's hand seems to be coming out of nowhere. Just in time, I remember to offer my own. We end up clutching fingers awkwardly.

"Nice to meet you, Mr. Rose," I say.

He leads me into another book-filled room, with one big desk facing two smaller chairs and pictures of, I guess, famous male graduates on the wall.

"You've come here all the way from Minnesota?"

"It's worth the trip," I say, cribbing from my Wellesley interview. Mr. Rose has a mahogany-brown mustache that lends an intelligent cant to his face.

"How do you like going to high school in Minnesota?"

I am turned around. Isn't he supposed to be asking me why I want to go to Harvard?

"It has its ups and downs," I say, quickly shelving my ten why-I-want-to-go-to-Harvard reasons and groping for new material. "I have some good friends and some good teachers, but I would like to come out East for a change."

"Anything specific?" Mr. Rose's eyes are the color of strong coffee, and they remind me of Jessie's — the way Jessie listens to me when I tell her something important, how she is so intense with her listening that her eyes seem to try to hear too.

"I wouldn't mind being in a more diverse environment, one where being, uh, Asian isn't such an anomaly."

"I was wondering about that," he says thoughtfully. "Isn't Arkin a largely Scandinavian community — blond hair and all that?"

"It is," I say. "And every so often I am treated to a racial remark or two."

I am telling this to Mr. Jeff Rose, a person who has a hand in determining my fate at Harvard.

"How do you react to such remarks?" he asks.

"I usually ignore them. I don't think I can change these people's way of thinking," I say. "And sometimes I study for revenge."

"Revenge?" he says, probably having visions of me buying a machine gun and dispensing Rambo-type justice.

"The people who call me names don't study," I say. "I guess I feel I can use the negative energy to do something productive, like prepare to go to college while they're preparing to live in Arkin and work as dental technicians."

"What's wrong with being a dental technician?" He is smiling, but I hear the challenge in his voice.

"Nothing," I say quickly. "But it's not a life I'd like for myself, so I think of studying as a way to get me to college and away from those people."

"That's a pretty complicated thought process to go through when someone calls you a name," Mr. Rose says.

"The hurt from someone calling you names is complicated," I fire back. "It's not easy to make it go away. The olden times were simpler: if your name was ever smudged, you could just challenge that person to a duel."

"Right," Mr. Rose says. He is smiling under his furry lip.

*

"Whom did you have as your interviewer?" Michelle asks as we're walking back to her dorm after dropping Mom off at the Harvard Motor Inn.

"A guy named Jeff Rose."

"Oh, Jeff," she says. "He's good. He just graduated last year; he's very impressed by intellectually creative people."

"How do you know all this?" I demand. I wish she'd told me sooner. I don't know if I gave any intellectually creative answers today, but maybe I would have come up with some.

"Richard worked in the admissions office this summer," she says. "And Jeff was getting trained, and they became pretty good buddies."

Richard, her boyfriend, had come out to dinner with us.

I've met him a couple of times, but I don't feel that I've
gotten to know him any better because he's so quiet. He
does seem nice, though. His hair is cut short and is sea-
urchin spiky, and he wears round wire-rimmed glasses that
make him look like an accountant. He spoke to Mom in
Korean at dinner and she blushed, saying her Korean was
kind of rusty.

"Can you give me any other hints?" I ask. Michelle looks
at me like a queen bestowing a favor.

"Richard says they've started having unofficial quotas
for Asians," she says. "Now the word is that you have to
get over seven hundred on your math SAT's, or you're
out."

I groan. "Can I do anything to study for it?"

"Buy a practice book — I'll give you the name of one —
and do the practice problems," she says. "Oh, and memorize all the vocab words for the verbal section. That'll give
you a good start."

We have reached the door of Michelle's red-brick dorm.
She fishes out her key.

"Any other hints?" I ask her hopefully.

"Yeah. For your achievement tests, take Math Two and
not wimpy Math One."

I'd already signed up for Math I, but I know I'll have to
unsign myself. I'd beg for alms in Harvard Square if it
would improve my chances of getting in.

*

Michelle has yet another test to study for, so we head to the
library. On the way out of the dorm, we are passed by two
guys in HARVARD HOCKEY Windbreakers. They are carrying cans of beer and one of them burps loudly.

"It looks like they're in for a hard night of studying," I say.

"Harvard is a very diverse environment," Michelle says, a little snappishly.

We spend a good three hours holed away in the bowels of Widener Library. I study calc, but the problems don't seem any easier, even here at Harvard. I wouldn't mind talking to some more Harvard students about how they like it here, but I see now that the idea is for me to get in first and like it later.

The next day, Mom and I drive to Providence, Rhode Island, to see Brown.

My Brown interviewer is nice — with her straightforward manner, she reminds me of Mrs. Klatsen.

"What kind of personal goals — that is, not the usual I-want-to-help-people ones — do you think you will achieve by being a doctor?" she asks, and I really have to think.

Among other things, I tell her, I want to try to achieve the high educational levels and the discipline I see in my father.

If she is surprised by my answer, she doesn't show it, but smilingly jots a few things down while still keeping an eye on me, like a gymnastics judge.

My overnight host is a jock named Betsy, who wears her brown hair in braids, like a little kid. She takes me to see the gymnastics facility, even though I'm pretty sure that I'll be retired by next year.

"Wow," I say when we enter the huge gymnasium. This place looks as if it's set up for the Olympics: a set of rings suspended from the ceiling, a big padded floor mat — unlike our thin one that curls at the edges — vault springboards that have air bubbles instead of the harsh springs, and two padded beams that are out of this world.

"This is nice," I say, patting the beam as if it's a horse. Rolling bare bones on this beam would feel so much better than on our plain wooden one.

"Actually, athletics at Brown aren't that great because they don't get the money some schools do, say Harvard or Yale, where the alums are constantly pushing more money in," Betsy says. She is on the crew and track teams. "But it's a good way to meet people and let off steam from studying."

I still can't get over this nice equipment, though. It seems that if you get into a good college, there are a lot of excellent things waiting.

For dinner, we go to a big dining hall, which Betsy calls the Ratty. We sit with a bunch of girls. None of them are in skirts — and a lot of them aren't even wearing make-up — but the conversation is a lot like the one I heard at Welles-ley: boys. I am beginning to think that intellectual mealtime conversations are just something that the school catalog people wishfully make up. I could live with that, though: while all the people I've met on this tour have been smart, they seem to be normal people, just like Jessie or Beth — or me? — which gives me some hope.

*

Mom and I fly home older, maybe wiser. We skip our sandwiches, which appear to be made of the same gray meat we had at dinner, and eat our brownies instead.

I still don't really know how I feel about the colleges; I think I could be happy at any of them. But then, is the question where would I be happiest going or where would Mom and Father be happiest sending me? I guess everything would work out quite nicely if I got into Harvard.

"Thanks for taking the time to bring me out here, Mom," I say. Mom smiles, a few brownie crumbs clinging to the corner of her mouth like dirt. I wipe them away.

"It was my pleasure," she says. "Hopefully, you'll be inspired now in writing your applications."

Applications, SAT's, gymnastics, calculus, grades. I'm going to have to sit down and clear out the clutter from my mind, or else I'm probably going to let something important pass me by.

I look out the window. Big, colored patches of land lie sprawled below me, a quilt over which the plane is slowly moving, back to Minnesota. I can see the plane's shadow on the land, and it appears to be barely moving. Yet, if we were closer to the ground, the plane would be moving almost faster than the eye can see.

✎ Ten

"CLEAR OFF YOUR DESKS," Mr. Carlson says gleefully as he begins to pass out our next calc test. "No rubbernecking — and Beth, no necking."

Every time we have a test, Mr. Carlson says his famous necking line to either me or Beth. We both hate being the only girls in the class.

When the dittoed test plops on my desk, all my inner alarm bells go off. I can hear Michelle, Mom, and Father chorusing: "If you want to get into Harvard, first you need good grades." I grip my pencil tighter.

"Okay, students, go to it."

Twenty-three pencils hit the papers with a resounding *thok-scribble-scrabble.*

I scan the first problems, but nothing clicks. Already, Beth's head is determinedly close to her desk, and she is writing furiously, an arm curled protectively around her paper.

When I move down to the story problems — "Say we are on another planet, where the laws of physics follow the principles of integral calculus" — they are a complete mystery whose secret is locked away somewhere.

With my stomach tightening, I move back to the short-answer problems, which are worth only two points each. But as I stare, the figures sprawl crazily before me, exponents rising and swimming away like protozoans.

I try to remember how to integrate. Finally, I recognize one of the problems as being similar to one we had for practice. I disassemble it, and the answer slowly forces itself into place.

After solving the first one, I crack the next ones like nuts, lining up the solutions neatly in their boxes and leaving the debris of my thought processes in the margins.

I check my watch and see how the precious minutes have slipped by. I jump to the story problems, but they still seem as mysterious as the Dead Sea Scrolls: "If two trains are approaching each other at x miles an hour . . ." I don't even have a clear idea of how to draw a little diagram of the trains approaching each other.

I move back to the short-answer problems to check them, and some of my new answers don't match. Is it the checking, or was I wrong the first time? My pulse speeds up.

I frantically do the two-point problems over again — and again — until I arrive at a consensus with the answers.

I hear a chair scrape. Beth rises and walks up to Mr. Carlson's desk and places her test on it. Mr. Carlson smiles at her, his eyes crinkling into little raisins.

I hear another chair scraping, and my hand freezes on my pencil. There are fifteen minutes of class to go. If people are already getting up, I'll never be able to concentrate, feeling like such a slowpoke.

My left hand, I notice, is curled into a fist on my lap. I open it and see the tracks of red, crescent-shaped nail marks running down my palm.

I stare hard at one of the stubborn story problems, waiting for a mathematical epiphany. I wish I could just shake the answer out, like a marble, from my brain. Doggedly, I try to at least set up each problem.

"Five minutes, class," says Mr. Carlson. Everyone is getting up now.

I flail and flail, drowning in figures and words that have suddenly become unfamiliar.

"Time to hand 'em in," Mr. Carlson says.

I surrender my test. My nose is warty with droplets of sweat, and I sigh. The good thing about tests is that they have to end eventually; the bad thing about grades is that they stay with you forever.

*

I drop my calc book, as though it were leprous, into my bag before heading to gymnastics.

Even on the mat I can't get calc worries out of my mind, and I am fervently praying that I'll get partial credit for the story problems I set up but didn't solve.

"Hey, ching ding-a-ling — watch it!" Marsha Randall's voice reverberates through the gym. I am standing, with my thoughts, in the middle of the mat, in her way.

I step off the mat with leaden feet. Everyone else is looking away, like that day on the bus. I hear the hollow *thunk-thunk* of someone working on the bars. Satisfied, Marsha zooms down the diagonal to do a tumbling pass.

I gather my sweats and walk out of the gym, anger and

sadness mixed inside me like oil and vinegar. I hear laughter spilling from the gym, and it all sounds so foreign.

I park myself, sweats and all, in Barbara's office. It's time to let her know that things have gone too far.

Amidst all the sports trophies, I sit on the hard wooden chair by her desk. There is a picture on the wall in front of me of Marsha Randall, smiling on the beam. I turn the chair so I won't have to look at it.

Beth is the first to pass the office on her way to the locker room. She gives me a smile of encouragement but doesn't stop. Marsha Randall and Diane Johnson flutter by, laughing and chattering as loudly as a bevy of quail. Neither glances at me when she passes.

Finally, Barbara comes in, lugging the heavy vault springboard. She stands it against the wall and then looks at me.

"Can I help you?" she says.

"Yes." I get up and shut the door. "I'd like to quit."

"What?" she says, looking at me as if I've gone dotty.

"I want to quit," I say. "I've had enough."

"What are you talking about?" she says.

Where has she been when Marsha Randall has been saying these things? On Mars? From her office, you can hear everything that goes on in the locker room.

"I've had enough of people calling me names," I say patiently.

Barbara looks at me. "Names?"

"Like ching ding-a-ling is not my name!" I have a sudden morbid urge to laugh.

"Ellen," Barbara says, putting her arm around me like a

sympathetic older sister, "I don't know what you're talking about — and you don't have to name names — but I'm sure they don't mean it."

"I think it's getting worse," I say, stiffening.

Barbara paces around the office, her huge body seeming to fill the small room. "Oh, you know how kids can be mean to each other," she says, rifling through some old score sheets. "Don't take it personally."

I feel my blood pressure rise. *Don't take it personally* — easy for her to say! I feel like yelling this to her face, but I let the stony silence of politeness take over.

"Listen, Ellen," she says, still rustling the score sheets. "You're doing really well this year, and I was thinking of putting you on as an alternate for floor exercise if we go to state."

An alternate for floor exercise? My ears unexpectedly perk up. That would mean a letter for sure.

"I don't want you to quit," she continues. "So how about it?"

My mind is swimming. Too much for one day.

"Well?" Barbara asks.

I remember how much I love gymnastics. I remember how proud I was the day I did a Valdez on the beam. I remember all the times I've envisioned myself in an emerald green letter jacket. I can't quit, I decide, just because Marsha Randall wants me to. If I quit, that would be one more triumph for her.

"All right," I tell Barbara. "I'll stay."

*

That night I am slogging through more calc problems, trying to see where I went off the road during the test. Jessie is probably at home listening to music or watching TV. Isn't that what the teen years are for — to hang out and be mellow? I never knew there was going to be this much stress or this much homework.

"Ellen, phone for you." Mom's voice is muffled against my closed door.

I flop onto my parents' bed and grab their phone. When I pick it up, I hear the click of Mom hanging up downstairs.

"Hi, Jessie," I say. "You're calling early tonight."

"This ain't Jessie," says a deep voice in my ear. "This here is Tomper."

I grip the receiver a little tighter and sit up.

"Hi, Tomper," I say. "What's up?"

"Not much," he says. "I just wanted to know if you've done the vocab assignment for English."

"No," I say. "I'm scheduled to give my book report tomorrow."

"Oh yeah," he says. "What'd you read?"

"*The Bell Jar.* What'd you read?"

"Nothing yet. I go next week."

I can't decide if I should be thrilled about his calling me or not. Lately, I've tried to give up on him, since I see him a lot at Marsha Randall's locker — which means that they're probably going steady.

"Well," he says. "At least you don't have to worry about the vocab assignment."

"Yes," I say.

"Well, I guess I'll see you around," he says.

"Yes, see you."

"Okay, bye."

"Bye."

"See you later, Gator."

"Would you hang up already?" In spite of my uncertain mood, I feel lightened.

"Right, Gator," he says.

"Goodnight, Tomper," I say.

*

When Mr. Carlson hands back our tests, I can't look at mine. I keep it face down and eye it warily; it's like a bomb that might explode.

I crane my neck until I can see Beth's score. An A sits like a happy tepee at the top of her paper. Maybe, by some act of God, the real answer to the story problems is that they are all unsolvable.

I lift the corner of my paper. A D-plus? How can that be? With all my troubles, I've never even gotten a C in here.

"How'd you do?" Beth asks me cheerfully.

"Awfully," I say, whipping the test back over. I listen closely, to determine if I can hear the doors to the colleges slamming in the distance.

*

From calc, I have to move right to English, where everyone is bustling more than usual because it's the first day of our oral presentation of book reports.

"I heard Mike Anderson tell Marsha Randall that he just copied his out of Cliff Notes," Beth says to me, her nostrils flaring with self-righteous fury.

"I believe it," I say, although it seems silly of him because Mrs. Klatsen gave us the option of reciting a memorized passage from the book or just writing a summary and reading that; it can't get much easier.

Marsha Randall goes first. She dramatically flips her hair back before reading her summary of *National Velvet*.

"Teenage Velvet was like any other girl who's horse crazy," she reads, bending her platinum head close to the sheet. "But who else would dare chop off her hair, don jockey's clothes, and enter the world's most grueling steeplechase?"

Beth looks at me and rolls her eyes. "That's from the summary on the back of the book," she whispers to me. "I know because I read it."

"Mike, you're next," Mrs. Klatsen says.

Mike walks up to the podium, sets his paper down, and then squints at it as if it's a script and begins.

"*The Lilies of the Field* deals with the interesting juxta . . . juxtapositioning of Homer Smith, an ex-GI on the open road, and Mother Maria Marthe, a nun topped off with the disposition of a drill sergeant."

I look over at Mrs. K., who is sitting impassively, with a slight smile on her lips. I wonder if she is concerned about people like Mike and Marsha who try to sidle through high school without bumping into anything that might work their brains or teach them something.

"Ellen, you're up," is all Mrs. K. says when Mike is done. I leave all my things on my desk and walk up to the front of the room. Twenty-four pairs of eyeballs roll to stare at me. I clear my throat.

"This piece is from Sylvia Plath's *The Bell Jar*," I say, surprised at how clear and resonant my voice can be. "I picked this passage because it captures the mood of the narrator slowly becoming depressed." I fold my hands in front of me, forget everyone, and speak. Before I know it, I am done.

There is a loud noise as people break into applause; I'm back on earth. Mrs. K. is beaming. Feeling my cheeks begin to flame, I return to my seat.

"That was beautiful, Ellen," Mrs. K. says. "Class, you should all take this as an example of a good reader and a good writer interacting. Ellen has managed to pick out a particularly sensitive piece of prose, and her delivery was excellent."

"You're a bomber," Mike Anderson says admiringly to me. Mike Anderson, admiring me?

After class, I start walking to my locker, and Tomper follows. "Your report was really good, Ellen," he says.

"Thanks," I say. "It was just memorization."

"No, you're really smart," he insists. "And you care about what you do."

I look at him. He's just read me like a book — and I like what he's seen.

"Thank you," I say. "And you're very smart, too."

"In what way, I'll have to find out — because it sure isn't gradewise," he says, his eyes studying my face.

There is a cord of tension between us that is being stretched tighter and tighter. Who knows what will happen when it breaks?

*

"How did you do on your calculus test?" Father asks at dinner.

My fork accidentally drops. I bend down to the floor to pick it up.

"All right," I say, carefully wiping it off.

"Did you get an A?"

"No."

"What did you get?" Father's voice rises.

"A B-plus," I say, crossing my fingers. "It was a hard test."

"B's aren't good enough," he says. "I think you'd better stay in and study until your grade gets back to an A — that means no gymnastics, either."

"No gymnastics?" I echo.

"No gymnastics." The tone of his voice makes me stop in my tracks.

"Yes, Father." What would he have done if I told him I'd gotten a D-plus? I must be the only kid in school whose parents are like this. Now, how am I going to earn my letter, or get to go out with Jessie, or do any of that?

✍ Eleven

"THE NEXT DAY, I ask Mr. Carlson if I can get extra help from him during lunch hours.

"Sure — you must have been having a bad day during the last test, huh?"

At our first meeting, Mr. Carlson opens a foil package and takes out a pastrami sandwich, the meat hanging out of the bread like a frill.

"Let's go over integration again," he says, then takes a bite and chews. "This is the building block of calculus," he says around his food.

He maps out the basic integration principles in handwriting that is surprisingly clear given his sausagelike fingers. At the end of the session, I have three new calc road maps, slightly stained with greasy fingerprints, to take home and memorize.

*

In gymnastics, Barbara thinks I've gone crazy.

"First you want to quit, now you want to stay on but skip practice because of your homework?"

I squirm. "My father suggests I stay out of gymnastics just until I do a little better in my math class — maybe only three weeks."

Barbara looks at me sternly. "I don't know about this, Ellen," she says. "I can't guarantee your place on the team."

"I know you can't," I sigh.

"I hope I see you soon, Ellen," she says.

I leave her office and try to block out all the gymnastics noise coming from the gym. I make the cold trek home, because I've missed the bus, doing my best not to cry, because the tears would probably freeze.

*

"Are we going to the hockey game tonight?" Jessie asks me on Friday when we're at our locker. Just the other day, I heard Marsha Randall congratulating Tomper for having been voted co-captain of the hockey team.

"Jess, I can't," I say. Jessie's eyebrows rise.

"My parents are really on my case about my calc grade," I say. "I'm sort of grounded — no gymnastics even."

"Grounded? What are you getting in there now?"

"A low B, I guess."

"Holy moley." Jessie slaps her hand against her forehead. "They're grounding you for having a B average? That has to be unconstitutional."

"It's this Harvard stuff," I say unhappily. "All this attention to grades. My parents will kill me if I don't get all A's."

"Harvard." Her face turns dark. "It must be one hell of a nerdy place."

"Are you mad at me?" I say.

Jessie drums her fingers on the locker door, then on her chin. "At you, no. At your parents, a little. No offense, but not only are they punishing you, they're also punishing me. I can always get Shari — Miss Party Animal — to go with me, but it won't be half as fun without you."

I sigh. I don't feel like studying tonight anyway.

Jessie looks at me, and she gets that soft look in her eyes. "Cheer up," she says, hugging me a little. "Did I tell you that I might have a crush on Mike Anderson?"

"Mike Anderson?" I say, momentarily forgetting my misery. "I would never have guessed that one." Jessie's cheeks are pink.

"We'll have to go to more hockey games, then," I add.

*

"I want to read your applications before they go out," Father says to me. His outline looms, like the Grim Reaper, in my bedroom door.

"What?" I say, before I can think to be polite. Luckily, at this moment I am studying calc.

"You heard me," he says. "I did it for Michelle, and she was very grateful."

For Michelle. Of course she would be grateful: her essays were perfect. Why does Father have to monitor everything I do, as if I'm going to become a delinquent if left to my own devices? I already asked Mrs. Klatsen to help me with my essays — what can he possibly catch that she, my English teacher, can't?

"Yes, Father," I say, because there is no other answer.

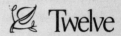 Twelve

"THIS ESSAY IS REALLY excellent," Mrs. Klatsen says to me during our after-school meeting. "Especially the epigraph: 'Like Homer's Odysseus, my parents set sail from home to a new land. Maybe like Odysseus, one day they'll return home. But where will I go? Born on the journey, I'm not sure where I belong.'"

I feel the red hands of a blush creeping up my cheeks. "Well, you've really helped it come this far," I say.

"You're a very good writer, Ellen," Mrs. K. says. "Have you thought about studying literature in college?"

"No, I want to be a doctor."

"You could study literature and still be premed — that's the beauty of a liberal arts education," she says, sitting up on her desk and letting her long legs dangle. "In fact, there are a lot of doctor-writers that you might like to read, like Walker Percy or William Carlos Williams — or even Anton Chekhov."

"Wow," I say, trying to digest everything at once. "Do you think there's a chance that I'll get into Harvard?"

"Ellen," she says, squinting to look at my face, "why do you think Harvard is the only place in the world?"

My cheeks flame up again. I must sound so pushy — so desperate.

"For one thing, it'll make my parents happy," I mumble.

"But what will happen if you don't get in?"

"I really don't want to think about it," I confess. "Where did you go?"

"Macalester," she says. "The little college in Saint Paul."

"And you liked it?"

"Loved it," she says. "There are a lot of places where you can study literature and biology, and that includes Brown and Wellesley."

"Yes," I say, but I am still thinking of my parents.

*

Right before Christmas vacation, I send all my application papers in. Father actually lets them go without comment. Did he feel uncomfortable reading about himself and my feelings on the page — especially one that's to be read by the distinguished admissions people? The whole time he was reading my Odysseus essay, his lined (yet scarless?) forehead did not budge. Maybe I was hoping the essay would touch him on a deeper level. But all he said was "There are no mistakes, Ellen, that's good."

*

Do you have to stay in and study *again*?" Jessie asks the next Friday night.

"Sorry," I say, although I could easily disobey because Mom and Father are out of town for the weekend. "Anything exciting going on?"

"Not really," she says. "Supposedly there is something going on at Rocky Jukich's house, but I heard that on Monday and haven't heard anything since."

"Well, maybe you can come over tomorrow, and we can make a snowman and drink hot chocolate," I say. "That's staying in — for me, at least."

"Okay," she says, brightening. "See you tomorrow."

Jessie is probably going to go out with Shari and have a great time. When will it be my turn to go out and have fun, the way teenagers are supposed to do?

I dig out a box of Kraft macaroni and cheese for dinner. The first time I ever made this, Father scowled and noted that only in America can you cook a dinner out of a box. I think the whole concept — not to mention the neon-orange color — annoys him.

Naughtily, I eat my dinner straight from the pot — to save dishes — and I read while I eat, which is another thing I'd never do if Mom and Father were home.

After dinner, I make myself a cup of instant coffee. I'm mad, but full, and I settle down to study.

At about 9:00, the phone rings.

I pick it up. The noise of traffic and wind rushes in the background.

"Hello," I say, putting my finger on the hang-up knob, just in case it's an obscene phone call.

"Is Ellen home?" A male voice. More sounds of the wind.

"This is," I say carefully, making a mental note to be sure not to mention that I'm home alone. "Who's this?"

"Oh, hi, Ellen — I can barely hear you. It's Tomper."

My finger falls from the hang-up knob.

"How are you?" I say.

"Cool," he says. "Just calling to see if you know of any parties."

Right. Calling me for party information is probably about as helpful as asking Mrs. O'Leary for fire prevention tips.

"Uh, how about the one at Rocky Jukich's?"

"That one never happened," he says.

"Well, the only other one I can think of is the wild one over here."

"Oh, yeah?" he says, suddenly full of interest.

"I'm just kidding," I say quickly. "My parents have gone to Minneapolis for the weekend, and I'm just hanging out." So much for my resolution.

"What if I came over to visit you? I've never seen your house before."

"Well," I say, then I hear a squawk on the line.

"Hang on," Tomper says. "The operator's asking for more money. Lady — I haven't got another dime."

I hold my breath, thinking of the fragile connection between Tomper and me.

"Hey," he says. His voice resumes, clear. "This thing takes quarters."

"Uh-huh," I say.

"So what do you think?"

My brain feels as if it's somewhere else, not in my head.

"Uh, not right away — I need to run an errand," I say, my eye on the macaroni and cheese pot soaking in the sink. "How about in forty-five minutes?"

"Sure," he says, between incessant honks in the background. "I'll go grab a burger or something. Is it okay if I bring some beer over?"

"Uh," I say, trying to measure the possibility of Mom and Father suddenly deciding to come home. "All right."

"See ya in forty-five, then."

From the phone, I run to the bathroom, rush through a shower, put on deodorant and perfume, and then reapply all my make-up. Then I streak to my room and throw on my favorite lilac-colored sweat shirt.

From my room I run around, picking things up, washing dishes, and shoving the living room couch's pillows back into place. I wish I had a minute to stop and look at myself; I must look like such a spaz.

Finally, the house is in order, and Tomper isn't there. I sit down at the kitchen table and reopen my calc book. I have a test on Monday — my big chance to pull my grade up — but I just stare at the page. My thoughts spin around and around. Why am I doing this when I'm supposed to be studying? Even more, why am I doing this at all?

The doorbell rings, and I jump.

"Hey, Gator," Tomper says, grinning in the doorway. His hair looks like a halo again, backlit from the street lights.

"Hey yourself," I say and reach over to help him with the paper bag that he's carrying; I almost drop it because it's so heavy.

"My God, what've you got in here?" I ask, peering into the bag. Inside are two six-packs.

"You aren't planning to invite people over, are you?" I ask with a gulp.

Tomper's eyes crinkle. "Cheez, Ellen, of course not," he says. "You've known me all this time and you don't know how much I drink? I could have a six-pack for breakfast, easy."

"Oh," I say.

I put the beers in the refrigerator and then notice that Tomper hasn't followed me. He has lagged behind in front of the glassed-in souvenir case in the hall.

"These sure are neat," he says, peering in as closely as he can without touching his nose to the glass.

"My parents like to travel."

"Wow," he says. "What a great way to remember all the places you've been."

"I guess that's why they're called souvenirs," I say. "It's French for 'to remember.' "

"Hey, that's neat," he says. "I didn't know you spoke French."

"A little," I say. I thought everyone knew what *souvenir* meant.

"How about a beer?" he says.

"Okay," I say. What does he want to do here, anyway? Play Monopoly?

"Hey, what's this?" he says. He is stuck deep inside our refrigerator. He drags out a huge Mason jar full of Father's kimchi.

"Oh, that's just kimchi," I say. "Korean pickles — it's stuff my mom and dad eat." *Stinky pickles*, I want to add, but I don't.

"Can I try some?"

"I don't think you'll like it," I say quickly. "It's really spicy."

"I love spicy stuff," he says. "Please? I'll only take a little."

Oh, we have tons more downstairs, I almost say, thinking of the jars and jars of it lined up neatly on the basement shelves, but I don't want him to think that we sit around eating stinky things all day.

"If you really want to," I say, reluctantly, to his sincere and eager face.

He unscrews the cover and uses the fork I've handed him to spear a piece of the pickled cabbage. He sniffs at it like a curious cat, before depositing it in his mouth. He chews thoughtfully. I hold my breath.

"Hey, this is pretty good," he says. "Only it isn't all that spicy."

"Really?" I say. "All Mom and Father ever do is talk about how spicy it is."

"You mean you've never tried it?"

"No, but it's always around if I want to."

Tomper spears a generous piece from the jar and holds it out to me at face level. "Here."

"That's okay, Tomper," I say, as the wilted leaf, mottled with angry-looking red spices, dangles in front of my nose. The garlicky vinegar smell is starting to seep into my nostrils, so I hold my nose.

"Ellen," he says. "What's the point of life if you aren't up to trying new things?"

The piece of kimchi hangs plaintively in front of me. I guess it's not going to go away. Still holding my nose, I take a small bite. While I'm chewing, I let myself smell a little. The taste isn't so bad — it's pleasantly garlicky. A second later, it sets my mouth on fire.

I run to the kitchen sink. It takes a full glass of water to put out the fire.

"Oh my God, that was hot," I say, thankful my seared tongue still works.

"It's not hot." Tomper laughs as he eats the remaining piece on the fork. He screws the top on and carefully puts it back in its place in the refrigerator, next to the milk.

"Aren't you going to give me a tour of the house?" he says, a little devilishly. My stomach quivers, and I gulp my beer. Then we head down the hall.

"This is a nice room," he says, surveying the shelves that have books lined up on them like straight toy soldiers. He pulls out the one that has the constellation Orion on its cover. *The Stars*, it's called.

"It's all about celebrities," I say. He has already cracked it open.

"You're such a goof," he says. "Where'd you get all these great books?"

"My father — he's always trying to get me and my sister to read more."

"I wish my parents were more into what I do," Tomper says slowly. "The only guidance I ever get is them telling me to stay out of jail."

"Stay out of jail?"

"Yeah," he says. "One of my brothers, Rick, was in jail once — D.W.I."

"How many kids are there in your family?" I ask.

"Just me and my two brothers," he says. "My brothers are both older: thirty-two and thirty-three." His eyes, now as blue as robins' eggs, focus on mine, as if he's searching for something.

"That's quite an age disparity," I say slowly, as if by cautiously letting out the line of my words I can haul them back in quickly if I need to.

"I think," Tomper says, drumming his fingers on his chin and keeping his eyes on me, "I think I was the little accident that came along way after they decided they didn't want to have kids anymore."

"Oh, Tomper," I say. "I'm sure they really love you."

"I'm sure too," he says. "But I also think they couldn't deal with the thought of having another bratty kid grow up in the house. I know I always felt that. You know, I learned to cook for myself when I was only five years old. I used to stand on a stool by the stove and make Rice-a-Roni." He puts his hands together and shakes them to demonstrate the proper technique.

"That must have been cute — you setting the house on fire," I say.

"Cute, nothing." His eyes crinkle wisely. "I had to eat." A lock of his blond hair falls into his eyes, and he brushes it away with a careless, impatient motion that lets me see him as a little boy.

"Here's Ursa Major," he says, opening the book. "And this clump here is the Pleiades."

The stars are so dense on the page that they look like salt spilled on a black tablecloth. With a practiced eye, Tomper traces out Orion's three-star belt.

"Take the book home with you," I say. "I don't think I'll feel like reading it again anytime soon."

"Oh no," he says, cradling the book in his hands as carefully as he might hold a puppy. "I might lose it."

"You won't," I say. "And keep it as long as you want."

A grin spreads across his face, like molasses making its way down a pancake. "Thanks, Ellen," he says. "You know I like the stars and all."

"Can I ask you something?" I say, feeling suddenly bold.

"Sure."

"Are you going steady with Marsha Randall?"

The words hang in the air for a few seconds.

"We've gone out a few times," he says slowly. "But it didn't quite work out."

"Hm," I say.

"Why do you ask?"

"I don't know." I want to say: "Then why don't you ask me out? You always act so interested, then you pull back."

Tomper slowly sets the book down and moves closer to me. Closer and closer — our lips touch. It feels so good to be close.

And because it feels so good, I push myself away from him.

"What's up?" he says softly.

"Nothing," I say, then it hits me. "Tomper, I really like you, but I think you have to make up your mind about things. You can't just come over out of the blue and expect me to be glad you want to kiss me."

A pause hangs between us like a heavy weight.

"I guess I know what you mean, Ellen," he says finally. "It's just so much simpler here, where it's just you and me. You're right, though — it's not fair to you."

I hand him *The Stars*, which he takes.

"Are you mad at me?" he says before he leaves.

"No, I'm glad you came," I say, and I am.

"Goodbye," he says. I can't help wondering if he means goodbye forever.

✒ Thirteen

O N MONDAY AT LUNCH, I try to eat some extra carbo-hydrates to give me energy for the big test. Mr. Carlson, between bites of his pastrami, patiently reviews the chapter with me.

"Ellen," he says, straightening up and mopping his brow, "you've done the homework problems *and* the extra ones I gave you. I'm sure you'll do fine on the test."

I give him the best grin I can, considering my nervousness, and I pull out the list of questions I've compiled. I'd much rather bother Mr. Carlson now than face Father later.

When I finally do get the test, I am surprised. This time I know what to do, and I have to keep myself from getting too scattered, like when I'm doing a crossword puzzle and know the answers faster than I can fill them in. I am done five minutes before the bell.

I sail, happy and confident, into English. Tomper comes in after me, but our eyes don't connect during the entire hour.

More of the same, I am thinking. I am glad now that I

didn't let him keep kissing me. It's time to go on with my life.

*

That Friday night, I show my parents my calc test, which has come back with an A, and I ask if I can go out with Jessie. They look at each other. Finally, Mom says, "Please be home by midnight." I give a whoop of joy and turn to the phone.

However, Jessie and I find ourselves without wheels. Father is on call and Mom needs the Blazer to go to a baby shower. Jessie's dad needs their car to go to his curling league game.

"Let's get dropped off at the Pizza Palace," Jessie suggests. "Maybe there we can go trolling for rides."

Mom drops us off, and Jessie and I take a booth near the door. We both order Cokes.

In a bit, a blast of frigid air hits us, and Rocky Jukich and a bunch of his friends walk in. Their faces are red with cold.

Jessie's eyes light up. "Hey, Rocky," she says, as they sit down at the booth across from us. "What are you guys up to tonight?"

"Nothin'," he says disgustedly. "A totally dead party scene."

"Mind giving us a ride somewhere, then?"

"Where you want to go?"

Jessie looks at me. I shrug.

"How about Erie," Jessie suggests. Erie is the next town over, where we occasionally go to shop.

"Okay," says Rocky agreeably. "Maybe things are more lively over there."

Jessie and I squish into Rocky's old Firebird. I have to sit on Jessie's lap.

"Anything particular going on in Erie?" I ask Jessie.

"No," she says. "But if it's boring there, we can always come back to the good old P.P."

The ride doesn't even take twenty minutes. The town is bigger, but not any nicer than Arkin. In fact, for some reason, Erie keeps its Christmas decorations up year-round, and year after year of Minnesota winters and baking summers leave bedraggled and sad-looking pieces of tinsel and fake holly twisted grotesquely around all the lampposts.

Main Street does have more stores, though.

"What clever names these bars have," Jessie exclaims sarcastically as we pass the Quart House and the Beer Hut.

"There's a place we go to sometimes that's pretty fun," says Rocky.

"Want to go?" Jessie says to me.

"We're underage," I remind her.

"They don't care at all," says Rocky, as if I'm such an amateur.

"Come on, it'll be fun," says Jessie.

I think of the alternatives, then decide, *what the hell*. This is my first night out in a while.

Rocky parks, we meet up with the rest of his gang, and we all troop over to a bar called the Watering Hole.

"Are you sure it's okay?" I whisper to Jessie right before we go in.

"No one in Erie knows us," she responds confidently.

We enter the bar, and no one stops us. A few people who are watching the Vikings game at the bar turn around, but I think they are only scoping to see who it is.

"Thanks for the ride," Jessie says to Rocky. "We'll catch up with you later."

Jessie and I make our way over to a raised area with tables and chairs. In the corner, a juke box brays out country tunes. We install ourselves at a table.

"What'll it be?" A girl in a halter top, tight jeans, and high heels has come up to us.

"A whiskey sour," Jessie says casually. I gulp and glance at the girl. She chews her gum impatiently, leans on one leg, and looks back at me.

"A whiskey sour, too," I finally choke out. I wait for her to slap the handcuffs on us, but all she does is write our order down and wobble away on her high heels.

The girl returns with two small cylindrical glasses, each with a skinny straw in it.

"I'll get it," Jessie says generously, as she hands the girl some money.

"Cheers," I say, and we toast. I take a tentative sip: it tastes like medicine. Now I wish I'd ordered a beer.

"A pretty good crowd," Jessie observes. Some guys have a fine red-orange layer of iron-ore dust covering their jeans and work boots. They must have come straight from work. Most of the women are in nice tops and jeans. The atmosphere reminds me of a grown-up Sand Pits party.

"Want to play some foosball?" Jessie asks.

"Sure." We make our way to the foosball table on the other side of the room. It is lit by a huge BLATZ BEER hanging lamp. Under it, two guys are already playing.

Jessie boldly clinks two quarters on top of the table. The blond guy farthest from me looks at her, then smirks at his partner, whose face I can't see.

The smirking guy loses.

"Damn, damn, damn!" he yells, spinning the goalie lever around and around in frustration. "Fucking shit, man!"

Jessie approaches the table, and I follow. The smirking guy makes a big show of letting us have the table, as if he owned it or something. Jessie ignores him and inserts the quarters into the table.

Jessie hands the first ball to me, and I push it through the hole, onto the "field."

Wham! Jessie sweeps it up and shoots it onto my side, narrowly missing the goal.

I am thinking: these plastic foosball guys are so weird. Head and torso painted with a doll-like realism, but the legs fused together into a peculiar peg shape.

While I'm ruminating over this, Jessie scores.

Plunk, plunk, plunk. I feebly try to get my guys to kick the ball out of the way, but I fail. Then again, I probably wouldn't be able to kick very well if I had those mutated club legs either. I take a sip of my sweating drink.

"You girls look like you could use some help," says the smirking guy to me. Under the light, the shaggy stubble on his chin looks like a porcupine's. He smiles, and I see that his teeth are tobacco-stained and slightly bashed in.

"No, thank you," I say politely to Ickyteeth, and I continue to futilely defend my goal. I make a lucky shot, then I accidentally knock the last ball into my own goal.

"Here, let's play two-on-two," says Ickyteeth, sidling up to Jessie. "We'll pay."

I expect Jessie to knock him clear into next week, but instead she smiles and says okay.

My mouth drops open.

"Hi, I'm Mitch," says Ickyteeth's partner, as he grips two of the handles on my side. There are four levers, so I can't possibly keep my hands possessively on all of them.

"What's your name?" he asks. He has brown hair and is better looking than Ickyteeth, but he does have acne craters all over his face.

"Jane," I mumble. I can't figure Jessie out. Why would she want us to play with these guys?

Ickyteeth and his friend Mitch start right in, as if this is the World Series Foosball Tournament. Ickyteeth almost slobbers with excitement, Mitch's arm muscles bulge, and both of them slam the levers so hard that the table shakes. A couple of times, Mitch's hip sort of brushes mine.

As usual, I'm a terrible goalie.

"Hey, man, we won!" gloats Ickyteeth. He puts his damp arm around Jessie's waist, and to my surprise, she acts as though she doesn't notice.

"Sorry," I say to Mitch, and I turn my back on him and head to our table. Then I see that all three of them are following. The two guys pull up chairs.

"What did you say your name was again?" asks Mitch.

"Ellen," I say. Then I remember that I said "Jane" earlier, but it doesn't look like he's caught it.

Ickyteeth grabs the girl in the halter top and orders another round of drinks. When it comes, I fish out some dollar bills and hold them out to him.

"Hey, no problem, Eileen," he says.

"I insist," I say, and mash the bills into his fist. I give Jessie a look to convey "When are we getting rid of these bozos?'' But she looks like she's having the time of her life: face all flushed, laughing at something Mitch is saying, hair looking vaguely Einsteinian.

I get up to go to the bathroom, and when I come back, only Mitch is sitting there.

"Where did Jessie and Ick — your friend — go?"

"To play another round," he says. I am suddenly aware of an annoying buzz in my head; I have no idea how long it's been going like that. Wearily, I sit down and sip my drink.

"So," says Mitch, glancing at me curiously. "You from China?"

"No," I say hotly. "From Arkin."

"No, I mean where are you *from*?"

"I was *born* in Arkin," I say. The buzzing gets louder. I try to change the subject. "So Mitch, what do you do for a living?"

"Work at Erie Taconite." He guzzles the rest of his beer while staring at me. I notice that his flannel shirt is soaked through. The mingling smells of sweat, old beer, smoke, and — faintly — laundry soap make me want to rush from the bar to the sharp, crisp air outside. Then he pulls out a cigarette and lights it, despite my polite coughing.

"You got a boyfriend?" he asks.

"Yes." I lie.

"Is he nice?" He blows columns of smoke out of both nostrils. For a second, he looks like a walrus. I start laughing uncontrollably.

"What's so funny?"

"Nothing," I sputter. My head feels heavy and light

at the same time. All I want to do now is go home.

"We're ba-ack." Jessie reappears, with Ickyteeth still surgically attached to her waist.

"Can we go?" I say. My voice sounds a million miles away.

"Sure," Jessie says, kissing the top of my head. "Gary, let's go."

"Huh?" I say, shaking my head. I can almost feel my brain cells floating in alcohol. "Where's Rocky?"

"Oh," Jessie says matter-of-factly, "he split."

"Wh-at?" I say in disbelief. "Our ride."

"Don't worry, Eileen." Ickyteeth leans close to me; his breath reeks of old hamburger and onions. "I'll give you a ride home."

"Oh, boy," I say in a tiny voice. What can I do? Call Mom and Father and have them pick me up at some bar in Erie? I swear that if I get out of this alive, I won't ever go out again.

Like a condemned prisoner, I follow everyone out to the street. Ickyteeth's car, at least, is a large, safe-looking Oldsmobile. Maybe I was unfair to expect a black Trans Am with skulls painted on the back.

Jessie and Ickyteeth get in front, and Mitch and I sit in the back. When we pass the last wilted MERRY CHRISTMAS sign on our way out of town, Mitch puts his arm around me. My first impulse is to push it away, but then I think about how I might hurt his feelings.

At a stoplight, Ickyteeth looks in the rearview mirror, sees us together, and cackles.

Thankfully, we go straight home. As usual, all the outdoor lights at our house are blazing.

"My parents are very protective," I tell Mitch as I fumble for the door handle in the car. "If I'm not home in time, they'll call the police."

"Really?" he says. Then he grabs my head and mashes his lips against mine — his sluglike tongue pushes roughly into my mouth, and I can't breathe. I push against him, but his hands are like a vise around my head.

When he finally lets me go, I gasp and sob for air. A vitreous bridge of saliva hangs between us. Jessie looks back, her eyes opening wide. Ickyteeth laughs.

Ickyteeth stops laughing when Jessie's fist hits his mouth. She jumps out of the car, flings open the door on my side, and pulls me out. Then she sticks her head back into the open door and say to Mitch: "You have ten seconds to leave, or you'll be spending the night in Arkin's jail. My dad's the police chief."

Ickyteeth, with one hand still over his mouth, already has the car in reverse. Mitch, however, sneers at Jessie.

"I'm not scared of you, bitch," he says to her. "Or you" — I know what's coming next — "chinkface."

He shuts the door in our faces.

Jessie and I go into the house. By some miracle, Mom and Father appear to be asleep and undisturbed by the commotion. Hot tears are already dripping out of my eyes, and I feel that I'm going to be sick. I run to the bathroom and throw up. Jessie comes in and holds my head.

"Are you okay?" she asks. When I lift my head, I find that I actually feel better, purged of everything — even tears.

"Jess," I say, low. "Can you stay over? If I take the

car out now, my parents might wake up and freak out."

"Okay," Jessie whispers back. "If it's okay with you."

Jessie quietly calls her dad, and in my room, I give her one of my big Sid the Killer shirts to sleep in.

"I'm sorry this night was such a mess," Jessie says, sitting tentatively on the bed. "I guess hooking up with those guys wasn't the smartest thing to do. They could have been ax murderers, for all we knew."

"Why did you do it, then?" I fight to keep my voice from boiling over. "Anyone could see a mile off that those guys were bad news."

"I don't exactly know," Jessie says gloomily. "I guess . . . I guess I was looking for some adventure — you know, sometimes I just want to bust out of this stinking little town so bad! I was thinking that maybe things'd be different in Erie, but that bar made me think of how things are gonna be if I stay here in this town and have to grow old with people like Brad Whitlock and Marsha Randall around."

Poor Jessie. All this time I've been making such a fuss about leaving, about going to an expensive school out East. I have a choice: my dad's a doctor, so he has all this money to send me all over the place. I never thought about what it would be like if I felt I was stuck in Arkin.

"I'm sorry — I'm to blame, too, Jess," I say. If I'm going to go to college next year, I'm thinking, I'm going to have to quit acting like such an immature little kid. If I didn't like being with those guys, I should have said something. Why was I waiting for Jessie to do something? And I should never have let that stupid Mitch lay one pinkie finger on me. It's about time I took some responsibility.

"Let's just pretend this never happened, okay Jess?" I say. "I'm going to take a shower and wash off all those Mitch germs."

"Better scrub," she says, smiling a little.

I make the shower as hot as I can stand.

✒ Fourteen

I FEEL HEADACHEY and awful the next day, and it's weird to think that Mom and Father don't have any idea that I was just in a bar in the next town, talking to strange men. Monday morning comes, like normal, and Father even says that I can return to gymnastics if I want.

Of course I go right back, but I find out that the season is ending early because we were beat out by Hibbing for a seat in the state tournament. I practice extra hard, and for the remaining meets, Barbara puts me on varsity.

A week after the last meet, we have our end-of-season party, complete with stale potato chips, in the gym.

Barbara calls us together so she can pass out the gold certificates, which we will take to Miller Sports to order our letter jackets. The younger girls watch enviously as Marsha starts the procession by getting hers, and then, since she's captain, calling the rest of the names.

People squeal and clap when Diane goes up to get hers — her third. People clap more politely for Beth. Barbara just passes out the certificates, like a disinterested Santa. Marsha goes down the line, then calls the last name.

It isn't mine.

Gretchen Wendell, a freshman who's been on junior varsity with me for most of the year, goes up, flushed and surprised, to get her letter. Everyone claps, and I follow mechanically.

When everyone starts talking and eating again, I grab Beth's arm and lead her to a corner of the gym where there's some privacy.

"Why do you think I didn't get a letter?" I whisper. Her certificate flashes seductively in the gym light.

"Ellen, I really don't know," she says compassionately.

"How does Barbara decide?" I am embarrassed at how desperate I sound. "How many varsity meets do I have to be in?"

Beth shakes her head. "I have no idea how she decides."

I glance over at Barbara. She is surrounded lovingly by her entourage of Marsha and Diane and all those girls. I couldn't break through the crowd now. Besides, this is supposed to be a party.

*

I know I can't rest until I talk to Barbara, but it's tough. I make up excuses for myself: it's almost the end of letter jacket wearing season, the jackets are expensive, I don't really want one.

Then I admit to myself that I really do want a letter jacket, and after working so hard these past years, it's not unreasonable for me to get one.

I keep heading down to Barbara's office at lunch and chickening out before I get there. Once I even bump into Barbara en route, like in some weird comedy; after we say hi, I keep walking.

"Ellen," Jessie says. "Nothing is going to happen unless you actually talk to Barbara. You don't get points for wearing out shoe leather."

"I hate confrontations." I groan.

"Try thinking of it from Barbara's perspective," Jessie suggests. "Say she somehow forgot your letter; she's not going to suddenly remember it unless you say something. Or say she didn't give you one because she's mean — are you going to let her get off the hook so easily?"

"All right," I say. "I'll do it."

I make myself march until I walk right into Barbara's office. She is there, eating a sandwich.

"Hi, Barbara." I try to sound casual.

She looks up, midbite, then puts the sandwich down. "Hi, Ellen," she says curtly. "What can I do for you?"

"Uh, I wanted to ask you why I didn't get a letter."

"Why you didn't get a letter?" she repeats. I nod.

Barbara heaves herself out of the chair and gets out her official score book, all the while looking at me as if I'm just a bit crazy.

"Ellen, you missed too many meets," she says, closing the book.

"But I was in at least as many — or more — varsity meets as Gretchen Wendell," I point out.

"Coming to practice counts too," she says. "I judge it on a person's overall commitment."

How much more committed could I be? I want to say. What about all those times I had to work extra hard so Mom and Father would let me attend practice?

Barbara looks at me as if she wants to get back to her lunch.

After school that day, I take the pictures of Mary Lou and Nadia off my wall. Next year no one will even know I was once a gymnast, because I won't have a letter jacket to show for it.

Michelle had said to me once that she didn't mind studying all the time because she had the feeling that if she just got all A's, everything would be all right.

I know that's not true now.

Getting all A's didn't get me the letter jacket I wanted so badly, and it didn't protect me from some bad men in a bar. What can grades do, except get me into Harvard? And there's not even a guarantee that they'll do that. I think of how all my life Mom and Father have treated good grades like the answer to life. They aren't.

I hope they know something I don't, I think to myself as I unstick the last picture and put it into the trash, along with all my emerald green letter jacket dreams.

✑ Fifteen

LETTERLESS, I ACE my final in calc.

"You're such an awesome brain," Jessie says to me after looking at the report card she's swiped from my hand. Since we don't have gym or swimming in senior year, my grade point is a perfect 4.0.

"You've got your A in music," I say. "That's great. Maybe you should think about going into music."

"Yeah, right," she snorts. "And I'll end up like Mrs. Matheny, left to teaching bratty kids like yours truly."

"What's going on here?" says a voice behind us. We turn to see Tomper standing there, grinning. Was he listening to us the whole time?

I discreetly take my report card back from Jessie and stuff it into my folder. Tomper is still smiling. I gather up my books.

"Are you carrying all that stuff home?" he asks.

"Yes."

"Well, here," he says, extending his arm. "Let me take them. I'm sort of walking your way — I'm going over to Mike's house to play guitar with him."

Jessie opens and shuts her eye in an exaggerated wink. I'd wink back, except I know Tomper can see my face. Could it be that he's made up his mind — in my favor?

We walk the road heading to my house. On the way, the bus passes us.

"How'd you do on your report card?" he asks. His arm swings my ton of books as if they are weightless.

"Okay," I say. My breath is silver in the cold. "How'd you do?"

"A new record," he says. "2.6."

I can't tell if that's a new high or a new low, but Tomper seems pretty happy. "Congratulations," I say.

Tomper smiles. His teeth are very white and straight.

When we get to my door, we stare at each other. I'm praying that Mom's not looking out the window at this moment.

"Uh, remember when you said that I needed to figure some things out?" he says.

"Ye-es," I say slowly, not daring to even hope.

"Well, I have." He grins. "I figured out that I want to ask you to a movie on Friday."

My face cracks into an involuntary smile.

"Why not?" I say. Trumpets play in the background.

"Good," he says. "We'll talk more at school."

He heads on to Mike's, and I float into the house — only vaguely worried about how Mom and Father will react.

*

When I show Father my report card, he nods and says "Good job, Ellen," in the same tone that he uses to say "thank you" to the person bagging his groceries. Mom, at least, keeps saying she is impressed. She makes my favorite dinner, real macaroni and cheese with big chunks of cheddar and Jenny Lee macaroni. She also hauls up an extra jar of kimchi for Father.

As we eat, I keep thinking that this is the perfect time to tell them about Tomper. But how do I break this? Father always talks so approvingly of how Michelle waited until she was in college to date.

I decide to just say that I am going over to Jessie's on Friday. This is going to be a sort of trial-run date, anyway — what if we don't get along? If something good happens, I'll tell them. But in the meantime, why risk the trouble? I have only one semester left of my senior year.

*

On Friday night, I drive over to Jessie's early. Tomper, thank goodness, didn't think it was odd that I'd want to be hanging out with her before our date.

"Here, this purple eye shadow will really bring out the colors of your eyes," says Jessie, playing make-up artist.

"Don't you think it's a little bright?" I ask. I turn over the case to see the name of the color. Sparkly Grape.

"Let me try it. I'll wash it right off if you don't like it."

"We-ell, okay," I say.

"You really have beautiful eyes, Ellen," Jessie says, sponging the color on my lid.

"I do?" I say, eyes still closed. When I think of my eyes, I think of a blah brown color, weird lids, and stubby lashes. Jessie has brown eyes, but hers are milk-chocolate colored, with lashes that curve gently outward like inverted clamshells.

"They have a ring of dark purple around the brown," she says. "Did you ever notice?"

"You're kidding, Jess," I say. "My eyes are so dark that they look like one big flat black pupil sometimes."

"No, look." Jessie scrounges around for a mirror. "The shadow brings it out."

I squint at my face in the mirror. The grape sparkles make my eyes look vaguely alien. I stare and stare at my brown irises. I think I might actually see a band of color around them, but if so, it's barely wider than a thread.

"Maybe you're right, Jess," I say. "But I don't know about this eye shadow."

"It definitely makes you look sexy," Jessie says. She sticks out her index finger and smudges each eyelid. "There, is that more subtle?"

My dark eyes stare back at me in the mirror. I've always thought light-colored eyes were more expressive, more precious, like gems. Marsha Randall's eyes would be emeralds, Tomper's would be sapphires, and even Jessie's would be citrines or something like that.

"You look beautiful," Jessie declares. "And it doesn't even matter. Tomper really likes you. I can see it in his eyes — he's gone."

Precisely at 8:00, a polite rap sounds at the door. Jessie and I both jump.

"You're going to have such a great time," Jessie says as she runs to the door. I hear it open, then I hear Tomper's voice and the stamping of feet.

"It's going to be a snowy one, Ellen," he says, shaking a few last flakes out of his hair.

"Right," I say, waiting for my voice to crack like lake ice when the pressure of temperature becomes too much. "Jessie's lucky she gets to stay in."

"You betcha," Jessie says, running to get my coat, just like a fairy godmother.

When Tomper and I go out into the fresh night, big fluffy flakes are wafting down. In a few seconds, I can see flakes hanging off my eyelashes.

"I wonder if this is going to be the last one this winter," he says, taking my hand and looking up at the February sky.

"I always like winter," I say, thinking how the lush carpet of snow covers everything with a glittery, clean whiteness. Even the air sparkles. New England winters, Michelle says, are blustery and gray.

We drive over to the Star movie theater, where Ghostbusters II is playing. The movie is perfect — not scary, lukewarm funny. Tomper and I finally kiss — warm, real kisses; it's a balm that eases those awful memories of the night in Erie.

After the movie, we go to the Pizza Palace, which is crawling with Arkin High kids. In fact, Mike Anderson and Brad Whitlock are at the table next to us — and staring.

"Hey, guys," Tomper says, as nonchalantly as if this were a hockey practice. I wave. Mike, at least, smiles back. Brad gapes as if Tomper is bringing in his pet tarantula.

Tomper and I order a pizza that's loaded with spicy pepperoni slices. I try to be ladylike as I eat and not make long mozzarella strings across the table.

After we're done, Tomper reaches for my hand. *I can't*

believe this is happening, I think for the millionth time.

He drives me back to Jessie's, where my car is parked, and helps me brush the snow off it. Flakes are still coming down.

"I had a really nice time," I say when we're finished.

"Me too," he says, putting his hands on my shoulders. I suddenly have this perception of him growing while I shrink — his huge hands swallowing up my tiny shoulders. Everything about him seems big, while I'm small and insignificant.

"I can see all sorts of constellations in your hair," he says, leaning close.

We kiss again, and again. The snow keeps falling gently around us; the air is cold, his mouth is warm.

He stops once to murmur, "I don't know what took me so long, El. I must be really stupid."

I silence him with a kiss.

✍ Sixteen

TOMPER AND I GO out the next weekend, and the next, and the one after that. I just keep liking him more and more — but I still carefully keep him away from my house, scared that Mom and Father's intervention could hurt.

One day after school, I go to meet him at his locker. As I come down the hall, I see that he is having an animated conversation with Brad Whitlock. I hear Brad say something like, "Why are you going out with her?" Then Tomper says, in a cheerful but firm way, "None of your beeswax, buddy."

They both shut up when they see me. Brad turns on his heels and leaves.

"Were you talking about me, by any chance?" I say uneasily.

"Hey, don't let Brad bother you," he says evenly. "He just has funny ideas."

"That's for sure," I say, but I still feel unsettled. Brad Whitlock is so popular that he could probably turn the whole school against me if he wanted to.

"Are you sure you don't mind?" I say. "You know, about me, us."

"Mind what?" he says, as if I'm crazy. "You're the best, smartest girlfriend I ever had."

I take him at his word, and even let him hug me before I start my walk home.

*

On the good side, even though I'm not exactly sure if my going out with Tomper has anything to do with it, Mike Anderson has been stopping by our table at lunch to chat with Jessie and me — and I notice that he always gets an extra twinkle in his eye when he's talking to Jessie.

"You'll never guess what Mike did," Jessie says as we park ourselves at our usual table in the lunchroom. She pulls out a music book. "He brought me Chopin's 'To My Friend Pierre,' which I've been dying to find," she says. "Remember how I kept calling Schmidt's Music and the boneheads there were no help? Well, he goes and finds it in this book in his Mom's piano bench."

"He knows about classical music?" I ask. "I thought he just played rock 'n' roll guitar."

"Oh, he's crazy about classical too," Jessie says as she begins to unpack her lunch. "He's the first guy I've known who doesn't think a sonata is a car."

"Or a treble clef something you get on your chin," I add.

Jessie giggles as she breaks into a bag of Cheez Doodles.

"Or a high octave a kind of gasoline."

Jessie throws a Cheez Doodle at me, just as Tomper takes a seat by my side. It bounces off his elbow like a tiny orange boomerang.

"Hey, cool it, girls," he says, but his eyes are twinkling. Our giggles are still spilling over.

Tomper looks grave all of a sudden. "Ellen, can I talk to you after school?"

"Sure," I say, panic rising from my stomach. "Is anything wrong?"

"I just need to talk to you," he says. Then he smiles, as if trying to lighten the moment.

"Okay," I say, my appetite flying away. "I'll wait for you."

When he leaves, I am gray with apprehension.

"Jessie, what could he want?" I moan.

"I don't know," Jessie says, handing me an "Almost Home" cookie. "But you know you can handle it, whatever it is. Look, you got all A's, so how complicated can a boyfriend be?"

*

Tomper is at my locker after school, and he still looks somber. Jessie has already gone to her piano lesson, so we're alone.

"Ellen," he says, leaning against the wall of lockers. I can smell his smell again, woodsmoke and soap. I grip the open locker door for support.

"Do you, like, like me?" he asks.

"Excuse me?" I say.

"Do you like me?"

"Of course I do," I say. The locker door is growing warm and sweaty under my fingers.

"A lot," I add.

Tomper takes a deep breath and then lets it out. "Then

why do you keep hiding me from your folks?"

"Huh?" I say.

"Come on," he says, looking at my eyes. "Tell me that you spend every Friday night at Jessie's and that you're always the one to pick up the phone at your house. Ellen, I thought you were one of the most honest people I know."

"Tomper," I say, "of course I don't spend every Friday with Jessie."

An "aha" look comes into Tomper's eyes.

"So you *are* embarrassed by me," he says.

"Oh, Tomper, that's not it."

"What is it, then?" he says, still staring at me intently. "You never let me get within ten feet of your house when your parents are home."

I sigh. Tomper has every right to be suspicious of me.

"I *have* been putting off your meeting my parents," I say. "But not for the reasons you think."

Tomper looks skeptical, but remains respectfully quiet.

"My parents are really strict," I go on. "My older sister didn't date until she went to college, and I have the feeling they want me to wait, too. I guess I was afraid my parents would tell me I couldn't date yet, so I decided not to take the chance of asking — because I like you so much."

Tomper rocks back and forth on his heels. "I believe you, Ellen," he says gravely. "But that's not the best way to go about it. Don't you think you owe it to your folks to be honest?"

"You don't know how strict they are," I say, finally releasing the door. The heat of my misery has fogged prints into it. "If they say no, it's no."

"I'd like to think I'm a pretty likable guy," Tomper says.

The janitor pushes his sweeping compound past us.

"Do you still want to go to the party Friday?" Tomper asks.

"Yes," I say.

He looks at me.

"Is it all right if I drop by your house at seven?"

"Okay," I say, finally, another knot starting to form in my stomach.

ℒ Seventeen

I SWEAT UNTIL Friday night's dinner. I show Mom and Father my A-plus chemistry test; then, with a gulp, I tell them that "my friend Tom" is coming over to take me out.

"Who is this person?" Mom immediately wants to know. She dishes a few spoonfuls of sticky rice onto my plate.

"Just a friend from school," I say, watching the steam rise off my rice. "The one who called about the vocab homework."

Father keeps his head close to his plate.

"Michelle did not go out with boys until she was eighteen," he says.

"I'm not Michelle," I say faintly.

Mom and Father look at each other.

"I don't think you should if Michelle didn't," Father says, keeping his eyes on his food.

"But Michelle didn't want to. I want to, and I got all A's." I stop with surprise. This is the first time I've ever argued with Father.

"Why would you want to?" Mom chimes in. "You'll meet a lot of nice boys in college."

My heart is sinking. I should never have let Tomper make me do this.

"Please," I plead, looking at my watch. "He's coming over at seven — maybe he's already left his house."

Father's face darkens, but he doesn't say anything. Mom dishes out more rice for all of us.

When Tomper arrives, a little early, I am sick with apprehension.

"Hello, Mrs. Sung," he says politely as Mom lets him in.

"Hello," Mom says back. "You must be Ellen's friend Tom."

"Yes," he says. "You have a very nice house."

Father is standing in the kitchen doorway. He is so tight-lipped that his mouth looks as if it has been drawn on. Tomper offers his hand, but Father looks at it like a foreign object. Then he looks at Tomper with a pained expression — as if he's just about to sneeze.

"Ellen needs to come in by ten," he says.

"Yes, sir," says Tomper, but Father has already turned away.

"Ellen, all your homework is done?" Mom asks.

"Yes, Mom," I say, as I usher Tomper out the door and over to his car.

"That wasn't so bad," Tomper says cheerfully.

I am sure I'm a picture of mortification. Why did Father refuse to shake Tomper's hand, as if he were some unsavory character? Did he dislike him because he could tell that Tomper wasn't an honor roll student, or was it just because he was some boy taking me out? Are they going to yell at me when I get home?

"At least they let me go," is all I can think to say.

We drive over to the Lakeview, to the annual hockey bash hosted by Mike Anderson's dad. The reception room is already crowded with the hockey team and the cheerleaders.

"I'm going to get a pop," Tomper says. "Would you like one?"

"Yes, thanks," I say, and I watch him walk away.

"Hi, Ellen." Marsha Randall is smiling at me. *At me?*

"Hi, Marsha," I say. "What's up?"

"I'm sort of bored now that gymnastics and cheerleading are over," she says, throwing a handful of her cascading hair over her shoulder.

"Uh-huh," I say. I can't figure out why she's talking to me. Is she sorry for the mean things she said to me before?

"How's Tomper?" she asks, touching my sleeve.

"He's fine," I say. It sounds silly, but it's hard for me not to like her when she's so pretty. "How are you?"

Just then, Tomper returns with our pops.

"Hi, Marsh," he says.

"Hi, Tomper." Marsha looks past him to the other side of the room.

"I think my boyfriend is waiting for me. Nice talking to you, Ellen."

Tomper hands me my pop.

"Who's her boyfriend?" I say, half to myself.

"Who knows? She's got a new one every week."

Tomper takes my hand.

"El, do you think we might leave a little early?" he says a little later. "It's nine already."

"Sure," I say, squeezing his hand. "My, how time flies when you have to be in by ten."

On our way out, Brad Whitlock and I accidentally bump into each other. He glowers at me and mumbles something that sounds like "fucking chink."

"Excuse me," Tomper calls out good-naturedly to Brad, "you gave Ellen a little bump."

Brad doesn't bother turning around.

"Did you hear him say something?" I ask Tomper.

"No, like what?" he says, his eyebrows raised.

"Oh, nothing."

*

Tomper drops me off a little before ten. He doesn't try to kiss me in front of the house, and I am grateful.

Inside, Mom and Father are getting ready for bed.

"Did you have a good time?" asks Mom, as I pass their room. I stop in the doorway.

"Yes. Thank you for letting me go."

Father is reading in bed, and he doesn't even look up. I feel scared for a minute, but then I realize I haven't done a thing wrong — why should I get the silent treatment?

"Good night," I say. *I haven't done anything wrong*, I repeat to myself. *I'm just asserting myself.*

𝒵 Eighteen

TOMPER AND I CONTINUE to see each other without incident, except that Father makes it a point not to talk to him. Mom, however, tries to be nice, and she even tells me that she thinks he's nice looking.

Pretty soon, of course, there are new worries. April Fool's day comes and goes, and the red-lined April 15 — college notification day — looms closer and closer.

I start getting bad stomachaches and can't eat. Mom worriedly makes me her cure-all, chicken-broth-and-rice gruel.

"You will hear from the colleges sometime in the next two weeks," Father says, as I listlessly try to spoon the gruel into my mouth. Today Mom has cracked an egg into it, so it is bright yellow.

"That will be a relief," Mom says.

What if I don't get in? That won't be a relief. I hadn't talked to God in a long time, but lately I've been praying every night — please let me get into Harvard or Brown or

Wellesley. I hope He doesn't get annoyed that the only time I think about Him is when I'm in trouble.

"Be sure to call me at the hospital the minute you know," Father says.

*

"Your Harvard letter came today," Mom says, as I gallop into the house. Today is April 17.

My heart sinks when I look at Mom. Why isn't she all excited?

"I didn't get in?" I say.

"I didn't open it," she says, a little shakily. "But it's thick."

"Michelle says they give out thick ones to the people on the waiting list, too," I say. My pulse is jumping all around as I pick up the large manila envelope with the crimson Harvard/Radcliffe logo on it.

Open it, I say to myself.

But things will be so final after I do.

Rip.

"We are proud to announce that Ellen Sung has been admitted to the Class of. . ."

I scream.

Mom screams.

"Myong-Ok, you did it!" Mom hugs me, and we jump up and down. I am laughing and sputtering and gasping for breath. I can't believe it — I really can't.

I look at Mom, and she has a tear in one of her eyes. She's so happy for me, but next year, both of her children will be gone.

We call Father at the hospital, and for some reason, he wants to know if I've heard from Brown, too.

*

The next day, Wellesley accepts me. A few days after, Brown tells me that I'm on the waiting list, but that my chances are quite slim because in their experience most people who are accepted end up going there. Figures.

Brown is out, I decide. I sit down, look at the Wellesley catalog again, and dig out Caitlin's number. Might I like Wellesley better than Harvard? I certainly think I preferred the close, comfortable feel of the campus. And how about classes with no dumb boys yelling out things all the time, like that guy Talbot Gray Suit will probably do if he gets in?

I call Caitlin, but she's not home, so I leave a message. The colleges are giving me a few weeks to decide, so I might as well take advantage of it.

*

"Why haven't you sent in your acknowledgment statement to Harvard?" Father asks me. I hadn't realized he was monitoring the family mail so closely.

"I haven't decided yet," I say.

"What's there to decide?" he asks, genuinely puzzled.

"Whether I want to go to Wellesley or Harvard," I say.

"Harvard is the most prestigious university in the world," he says. "There's no question about that."

I sigh. "But isn't it great that I have a choice?"

"Maybe between Harvard and Yale I could understand," Father says. "But you really perplex me sometimes, Ellen."

I gulp. Yes, it would be so easy. Just send in the card, do

· 134 ·

not stop, go to Harvard. All the college books say it's the hardest to get into.

"Father," I say. "I'll decide before the deadline, I promise."

*

"Harvard has one of the best med school acceptance rates in the country," Michelle says when I call her. "Also, there are a lot of resources in the graduate departments; I've had some bio tutors who were Ph.D. candidates, and they got me really interested in research. If you went to Wellesley, which is strictly a college, you might miss out on some of these advantages."

"That makes sense," I say.

"And Ellen, med schools are still much more male than female, so I think the sooner you start to slug it out with men in your classes, the better. Wellesley is a good school, but Harvard will set you up better."

"Hm," I say.

"Ellen," Michelle says, as if she's trying to coax a child, "send the form in — don't upset Father any more than you have already."

The form, the form.

Caitlin calls me back that night.

"My experience has been amazing," she says. "I can't tell you how much it's helped my self-confidence."

"That's good to know," I say.

"But, of course, single-sex education is not for every-one," she goes on. "If you're into meeting guys in your classes and stuff like that, you have to realize that you just won't do that here."

That is something I have to think about, I admit.

"Thanks for your honest opinion," I tell her.

Finally, I go to see Mrs. Klatsen.

"That's such wonderful news!" she says. "Which one have you chosen?"

"That's my problem," I tell her. "I need to decide — where do you think I should go?"

"Ellen," she says. "They're both such excellent schools, I don't think you can go wrong at either of them. It just boils down to your individual preference now."

*

"Remember when I was worried that I wouldn't get into Harvard?" I say to Jessie, as we lie in her room, listening to her new "Sid the Killer" album. "Now I'm an even worse basket case."

"Well, even though it's great that you got in, you're right not to go blindly just because everyone thinks you should. You should be able to look back and be happy, not like 'I wish I'd gone to Wellesley.' What's the use of living to a ripe old age if you have to carry regrets around?"

*

I take a long walk and think about regrets. I've regretted some parts of the way this year has turned out — mostly about Marsha Randall and Mr. Borglund and Brad Whitlock. And now, haven't I gotten what I've worked so hard for — the chance to blast out of here, to Harvard? I really have wanted this, haven't I? Maybe I was scared before that I wouldn't measure up to Michelle; but Harvard accepted me, just the way they accepted her, so I must be ready to do it. So I will.

put the acknowledgment card for Harvard in the mail. Father brings it out to the mailbox without saying anything.

One day, I think to myself, *I will figure out how to please my parents without silencing my own voice.*

✍ Nineteen

"BOY, I DON'T KNOW where this year went," Jessie says to me as we make up our faces for graduation.

"Me neither," I say. No more sharing lunch with Jessie, no more Mrs. Klatsen, no more seeing Tomper in the halls.

Jessie sprays her hair and sets the ill-fitting, slippery cap on top of her head. "Maybe we should use staple guns," she mumbles, her mouth full of bobby pins. I spray and spray my hair until it looks like a lacquered doll's.

Finally, we start our walk to the high school, both of us stepping tentatively, as if we're carrying big jugs of water on our heads. Jessie is clutching her pink Instamatic camera by its wrist strap. I didn't bring a camera because Father is so fastidious about documenting important family events.

At school, we meet up with Tomper, Mike, and Shari.

"You girls look very nice," Tomper says gallantly.

"God, I hope this goes fast," Shari says, a cigarette wiggling in the corner of her mouth.

"Hey, Ellen," says Mike, "aren't you giving a speech tonight?"

"I'm not the valedictorian. Beth is," I say. "Her grades were so impressive that Macalester gave her a full scholarship!"

"Here I am," says Beth, joining our group. "Fourscore and seven years . . ."

I put my arm around her and Jessie takes a picture.

Mr. Olson, the new assistant principal, sticks his head out the window and yells at us to come inside and get in line.

"Sheesh," Mike says. "Here we're done with classes, and they're still trying to order us around."

We saunter into the dusty school — one last time.

The line that's going to lead into the auditorium is alphabetical, but there are so many S's — Sanderson, Sasso, Suikonnen — that I'm not even within shouting range of Tomper. We are all packed right outside the auditorium door, rustling restlessly like cattle before a stampede.

Finally, we are given the signal to move. I can feel my mortarboard slipping already. I shove a hairpin in fiercely, and it scrapes my scalp.

Once we're seated in the reserved front rows of the auditorium, Beth walks up to the podium on the stage. The glare from the overhead lights makes her glasses look opaque.

"When we're thirty," she says, her voice sweet and confident, "the four years we've spent in high school will seem like no time at all. But all the friends we've made, the things we've learned — these things will stay with us."

Beth goes on to talk about sports and homecoming, about teachers who helped shape us, and about silly things that people did in the halls. I feel a lump form in my throat — I guess I'm more nostalgic about high school than I thought.

When Beth is finished, the applause is loud and deep, like the roar of the sea. Beth smiles shyly.

Then the school organ starts wheezing out the first bars of "Pomp and Circumstance." I can feel my hair stand on end. I don't feel ready to graduate.

Our line gets up, and we start marching toward the stage. The principal, Mr. Richtarich, is standing in the middle of the stage to hand out the diplomas. Mr. Olson stands to the side, calling out names.

As we march up to the stage, I look back into the audience to see if I can spot Mom and Father, but the rows of heads in the darkened auditorium look anonymous, like a carton of eggs.

This is Mr. Olson's first graduation ceremony. He is sweating under the hot lights, and when he starts calling the names over the microphone, he speaks so quickly he sounds like an auctioneer. Soon, there is a traffic jam of graduates around Mr. Richtarich because he can't pass out the diplomas fast enough. He turns to give Mr. Olson a reprimanding look.

Mr. Olson blushes and slows down.

When Greg Suikonnen steps from in front of me to get his diploma, my heart immediately starts racing. I watch him make his way down the stage and shake hands with Mr. Richtarich.

"Ellen Sung," says Mr. Olson.

I move toward the center of the stage, concentrating on walking not too fast or too slow.

"Chink!" hisses a male voice somewhere back in the line

of seniors. My feet freeze to the stage. Otherwise the auditorium is silent.

"Carla Sunnonberg," says Mr. Olson.

My legs start moving again, to my relief.

"Congratulations," says Mr. Richtarich, shaking my
hand. As if in a dream, I take my diploma and keep moving. All I want to know is who has ruined this night for
Mom and Father? Who?

After the ceremony, I push to find Jessie. The lawn is
packed with parents and kids moving in every direction. I
finally spot her with her father, and I run over.

"Jess," I whisper as I touch the sleeve of her gown, "did
you hear what happened when I went up for my diploma?
Someone in line yelled 'chink.' "

"Jesus," I hear her say as I turn away, suddenly having
spotted Mom and Father coming toward us. Father has the
camera raised and ready, so I start smiling stupidly.

"My God, Ellen," Jessie says to me privately after the
pictures have been taken. "I can't believe that happened. If
I find out who did it, they're dead meat, for sure."

Just then, Tomper walks up to us. He hugs Jessie and
kisses me on the nose.

"Tomper," I say. "Did you hear anything funny when I
went up to get my diploma?"

Tomper looks puzzled. "No, why? Did Olson say your
name wrong or something?"

"Oh, never mind," I could have sworn I heard a voice,
Brad Whitlock's voice. But why didn't anyone else hear it?
Am I becoming paranoid?

I ask Mom and Father if it's okay for me to go back to

Jessie's, where we'll change and then go to Mike Anderson's graduation party.

"Of course — stay out late," Mom says, beaming. "Myong-Ok, we're so proud of you." Mom kisses the top of my head.

"Yes," Father agrees. His expression is the same as usual, and I'm glad. I really must be hearing things.

We go back to Jessie's, change, and glop on more makeup. Then we head to Mike's.

Almost two hundred people show up to drink beer, eat Cheez Whiz artfully arranged on Ritz crackers, and otherwise pay their respects to Mike. It is way past midnight when I finally stumble home.

There is a single light on in the kitchen.

Father is sitting under the light. On the table are the two photo albums I found when I was snooping in his study.

"Uh, hi Father," I say, trying not to stare too hard at the books as I make my way to the stairs. When I look back at Father, he looks so still, so strange sitting under that pyramid of light.

"Myong-Ok," he says. "What happened to you tonight made me think of these books."

So it had happened — and they had heard.

"Oh, don't worry," I call lightly, from the stairs. "People in Arkin can be so ignorant."

"It's not just Arkin," he says. Something in his voice draws me to the table.

"When your mother and I came to this country," he says, looking at me gravely, "we were not prepared for the way we would be treated. People shouted at us, saying 'Go home Chinese!' or just made it clear that they did not like the color of our skin."

"Right," I say, trying to gather my wits — and reminding myself to pretend that I'm not already familiar with these books in front of me. "What are these books?"

"They are the few memories I brought back with me from Korea," he says. "I try not to look at them too often."

"Why?" I say, thinking of all the stories I wanted to know, all the Korean Michelle and I never learned.

"When you leave a country," he says, "it is like an animal caught in a trap that gnaws a limb off to free itself. You can't dwell on what you've lost — if you want to survive. You have to go on with what you have."

"Yes," I say, my ears wide open.

"When I was a little boy," he continues, "I used to stand outside the U.S. Embassy for hours trying to get a glimpse of those mysterious creatures, the Americans. They were always so loud and happy — they fascinated me. When I was at the university in Seoul, the American GI's would give the students magazines they were going to throw away. My favorite one was *Life*. The colors on those pages! More vivid than anything you could find in any ancient Korean books — and here were these people throwing these magazines away. I thought America had to be a very special place if you could do that."

"Especially wasteful," I say, but he doesn't appear to hear me.

"One day, I came across the most beautiful rose color," he says. "More beautiful than any flower I ever got for your mother. It was so beautiful that I tore it out and put it up in my little locker to inspire me to study hard — especially English. From that moment on, I knew I would be going to America — to *Life*.

"And now that I am here," he says with a sigh, "I can buy all the Chuckles candy — we used to call them 'jellies' when the GI's gave them to us — that I want. To think that those candies were like gems to me, once."

I swallow, and feel as if I have a piece of tissue stuck in my throat. "All in all, are you happy here, Father?" I croak.

Father looks at me and rubs his eyes under his spectacles. "I always hoped it would be better for you and your sister," he says. "You have gotten into the best school, and I am sure you will both become fine doctors."

"No," I say. "How about you? Are you happy?"

Father looks at me, and for a moment, I think I see the flickering of a sad smile.

"There were times when I thought I would be able to go on with my research work," he says. "But I soon realized that no matter how well a person is educated in another country, an immigrant must fight for work, especially if his skin is not white. It was lucky that my friend from the army found me this job here in Arkin, or we might have been sent back to Korea."

Sent back to Korea? Michelle and I would have been Koreans.

"Is that why you and Mom pushed me and Michelle so hard — so we could succeed in America?" I ask.

"That is much of it," he says. "When I went to high school, my parents sacrificed a lot so they could send me to Japan — at that time, all the best schools were in Japan. So

I studied hard and was accepted to Seoul National University, the very best school in Korea. Many of my classmates have gone on to become big people in business, in medicine, and so forth, in Korea. Yet over here, all people cared about was that my degree was not American, which in their eyes meant not as good, not as smart.

"So now," he goes on, "you and your sister can do more than I or your mother ever could: you will graduate with degrees from Harvard, and nobody can say anything to you, because everyone knows Harvard."

All this time I thought I was getting those grades for him and Mom. And Mom and Father just wanted to set me up for a better life.

For the first time, it really hits home that Mom and Father left a whole different country behind to come here. The change must have been frightening, and they must have felt alone and strange when they first arrived.

"Do we have any relatives here in America?" I ask.

"Most of your relatives are in North Korea." Father sighs. "And that is another story."

He turns the page of the album. The pink piece of paper is still wedged in the binding. The picture of the woman holding the moon-faced boy stares out at me.

"This is your grandmother," Father says.

I see a thin film of water on my father's eyes, but it evaporates quickly, like dew.

"Please tell me more about Korea," I beg.

I notice, then, that the first light of dawn has turned the kitchen gray.

✍ Twenty

AS THE SUMMER SETTLES IN, I do my best to enjoy my last set of lazy days before I start my college career. Michelle has never spent a summer at home: this year, she is spending it in New York doing some heavy-duty research project at the Albert Einstein School of Medicine, which sounds appropriate. I keep wondering from time to time if Father is secretly happy that Michelle is showing such promise as a researcher.

Michelle did send me a list of books she thought I should read before going, and it is pretty scary: a lot of these books I've never heard of, much less read. There's no way I'll get them all done this summer, so I just go to the library and pick out a few each week.

Really, though, especially since Jessie and Mike have started to go steady, I just spend a lot of nights out with them and Tomper — I feel it sort of makes up for all those nights I had to stay in studying during the year. Somewhat surprisingly, Mom and Father don't say anything — they just pretty much let me go my own way.

Tonight, I've gotten permission to stay over at Jessie's cabin. What I didn't tell them is that we're meeting up with Tomper and Mike to go to the drive-in's Buck-A-Load night. Buck-A-Load is a fun way to see kids from our class. Because going-out nights aren't restricted to weekends anymore and because party info is much more haphazardly disseminated, Jessie and I have fallen out of touch with a lot of Arkin High people, which really isn't all bad. I make sure I see Beth regularly, so there's no one I really miss.

"What's playing?" Mike asks, as we drive in.

"Texas Chainsaw Massacre Two," chortles Jessie.

"Ugh," I say. "Those kinds of movies give me nightmares."

"You'll have to get used to the sight of blood if you want to be a doctor," Jessie reminds me.

Inside, she parks but doesn't hook up the speaker. Without the sound, the movie picture flickers fuzzily, benignly on the screen. Jessie cracks open a pop and passes cans of Bud around.

"Compliments of Dad," she says. "Now that I'm a big girl, he says I can take anything out of his liquor collection as long as I don't drink and drive."

"Let's hear it for adulthood," Mike says, toasting.

We see Rocky Jukich and Shari walk by holding hands. Diane Johnson and some of the ex-cheerleaders — but not Marsha Randall — also go by. It's funny how we can observe everyone like this, yet none of the passers-by think to look in the car.

Brad Whitlock walks by next, carrying a huge tub of

popcorn. I mentally will him to spill it on his pants, but he goes by safely.

"There goes a dickhead," remarks Jessie.

"You can say that again," says Mike.

"I thought you guys were really good friends, Mike," I say, puzzled.

"We *were*," he corrects. He turns around and looks at me. "You know, Ellen, I've felt really bad ever since that day Brad called you that name on the bus."

"You still remember that?" I say, surprised.

"I remember that I should have said something then and there," he says. "But you know, Brad's the type who makes fun of everybody and everything, so it was kind of easy for me to think, well, he's just playing around — hell, he and I have been going to hockey camp together for years — so I let it slide."

"Nice going," says Jessie.

"I know," he says. "But then after I got to know you, Ellen, and saw what a nice girl you are, I started realizing that Brad really did mean a lot of what he said, that he really did hate, in a bad way. Then when he started pressuring Tomper —" Mike looks at Tomper as if he's not sure he should go on.

"Pressuring you about what?" I ask Tomper.

He squirms. "Like I said, El, Brad just has funny ideas."

"He wanted you to stay away from me because I was Asian?" I venture.

"Something like that," he says.

"We all three came to a kind of disagreement," Mike

· 148 ·

concludes. "Tomper was much more forgiving — I told Brad to go to hell.

"I guess what I mean to say, Ellen," Mike goes on, "is that I'm sorry I didn't speak up at the time — I should have."

"Don't worry," I say, feeling touched. "I needed to learn to speak up too."

In the dark, Tomper squeezes my hand.

*

The bunch of us go back to Jessie's cabin after the movie. Jessie and Mike immediately retire to one of the bedrooms, and I tentatively go into the one I usually use. Tomper stands in the doorway.

"I could sleep out here on the couch," he says. "Or I could sleep with you."

I look at him, and I'm stuck.

"I don't know," I say.

"I wouldn't mind being able to hold you — I'll be nice," he adds with a light laugh.

I nod, and he grins like a little boy just given fudge.

I go into the bathroom, brush my teeth, and change into an extralarge T-shirt.

Tomper brushes his teeth using my toothbrush and then joins me in bed, which sags like a hammock. He closes his big arms around me; the lumps of his muscles are hard even when his arms are relaxed.

"G'nite, Ellen," he says once we're wrapped in a cocoon of warmth.

" 'Nite," I say, already feeling sleep dragging me down.

Vaguely, in the other room, I hear the squeaking of springs.

*

The next morning, Tomper and Mike take off early to go fishing. Jessie and I sleepily putz around until noon. Jessie makes a double batch of macaroni and cheese, and we bring it outside — pot and all — on the porch. As we eat, we watch the lake swooshing and slapping the shore with a reassuring tempo. When Tomper and Mike got us up early this morning, the lake was still, like plastic wrap, with a soft mist rising off it.

"What're you going to do next year, Jess?" I ask.

"I guess go to business school in Duluth," she says.

"What about your music?"

"There's really not much more to do," she says. "I'll never be a concert pianist, and I don't want to teach."

"What's Mike going to do?"

"He's going to be at the U. in Duluth playing hockey."

"That's a nice coincidence," I say. "When's the wedding?"

Jessie blushes. "Actually, you know, the other day he said, 'When we get married, do you want to stay in Duluth or move back to Arkin?' He said it in his normal goofball way, but he sounded like he wanted an answer."

"Wow, Jess, that's great," I say, although I can't envision it for myself. I haven't even begun my four years of college yet.

"It's weird, though," she says, rocking her legs against the rough wood of the picnic bench we are sitting on. "I keep wondering: If we get married and settled, say in

· 150 ·

Arkin, is that all there is in life? I mean, there's got to be more to life than going to parties, shacking up, and having kids."

"There's got to be," I say, and for some reason, I move to sit closer to her. I want to remember Jessie and this very day, even when we're three thousand miles apart.

✑ Twenty = one

AUGUST DRAGS IN ON lethargic legs. But still, it all seems too fast, too sudden. Tomper and I have been spending a lot of time together . . . and sometimes my body has been telling me that I want to do more than what we've been doing — and I'm sure he does too. But we've both been hanging back, knowing that the end of the summer is going to mean the end of us. Tomper will be leaving Arkin too: he's going into the army, and he'll be off to South Carolina in the fall.

"You're leaving so soon," Jessie says, as we sit in my room. We are staring at the open box in the middle of the floor. So far, all that's in it is the new underwear Mom bought me and the Holstein clock.

"Well, it's only three months till Thanksgiving vacation," Jessie says hopefully.

"Four months until Christmas," I tell her. "Michelle comes home only for the big holidays because it's too much money and too much hassle."

"Oh," Jessie says, staring at the floor. "Ellen, let's go out to the cabin, get on the inner tube, and float into the middle of the lake."

I fish my swimsuit out of a drawer. "Let's go."

*

Two weeks before I'm scheduled to leave, Jessie, Tomper, and I decide to go to one last party, which Mike is having out at his cabin.

The party is mobbed with Arkin High graduates. Even Marsha Randall is there, flirting heavily with Mike and all the other guys at the party.

"I heard our friend Marsha couldn't get into dental hygienist school," Jessie says, as we're standing under the huge floodlights that Mike's father has put up in the yard. "Figures, for someone with the intelligence of Barbie doll cereal."

"Hm," I say. Marsha is now wrapped around some guy who is raising his beer glass to her lips, as if he were giving her communion.

Tomper walks up to us, only I don't recognize him for a second.

"Nice haircut," Jessie says. All his beautiful wild golden hair has been shorn off. My heart beats painfully.

"Do you like it?" He grins. "It's the army special."

"I thought they cut it for you," I say. Already, he doesn't look like the Tomper I knew in high school.

"They do," he says. "But my old man says it's good to get used to it beforehand — there'll be enough else to get used to later on."

Jessie and I decide to climb down to the lake, where we sit on the dock and watch the moon dance on the water. On

· 153 ·

the other shore, voices and laughter carry over the acoustically conductive lake, right to our ears.

"You're my best friend, Ellen," Jessie says in the dark. "I would've never survived this year without you — without you around to make me laugh."

"Make you laugh?" I say, surprised. "You're the wit."

"Hell," she says, skipping a stone on the water. "We're just a barrel of monkeys, aren't we?" I know we can both feel the white heat of summer fading and the fall closing in.

When we climb back up to join the party, Marsha Randall suddenly comes up to me and shoves me hard on the shoulder.

"Hey," I say. Her breath reeks of beer, mixed with the sickening scent of her perfume.

"Hey yourself, fucking ching chong Chinaman."

"What did you say?"

"Fucking ching chong Chinaman," she says in a high-pitched voice. "Chingchongchingchong — God-damn slitty eyes. You don't deserve Tomper at all."

Her twisted face is inches from mine, the rancid odor of her breath making me gag.

"You're so ignorant!" I shout, as if I've found my voice for the first time. "You are a racist idiot!"

Marsha comes at me, clawing my face and my clothes with her long fingernails.

"Hey!" I hear Jessie yell. Marsha's hands keep coming at me, nicking my eyelid, my cheek. I shut my eyes, pull my fist back, and punch with all my might. My fist connects with her jaw: I hear the sickening click of her teeth. She falls, in a tangle of hair, but she gets up, and I hear the breaking of glass.

The next thing I know, I am on the ground. Warm tears — although I don't feel myself crying — gently flow down my face.

"Oh my God!" Jessie sobs, kneeling near my head. "Ellen, please don't move. Hang on, hang on."

"I'm fine," I want to tell her, but I feel so tired all of a sudden. I wish everyone would leave me so I could go to sleep.

Next, I hear Tomper's voice, deep and warm. "Ellen, it's gonna be all right."

"I know," I want to say, but I'm so tired. Something soft snuggles up to my face, and then I realize I'm being lifted. I open an eye and see Tomper's chest. He isn't wearing a shirt. His skin, next to my cheek, is wet and sticky.

"I love you, honey," he whispers into my ear.

*

I am at the drive-in, but I see Jessie, Tomper, and Mike drive away without me.

"Wait for me! You forgot meeee!" I shout, but my mouth is funny and no sounds come out. I run after them, but the car is picking up speed. Faster and faster, it is heading toward a bright light.

*

My eyes snap open. I smell that funny hospital smell Father always has on him.

"Myong-Ok," Mom says, coming over to me and bending her head close to mine. She looks as if she's lost weight overnight: her face is as gaunt as a ghost's. "How are you feeling?"

"Fine," I say, but when I see her face, my eyes fill up with tears.

"Does anything hurt? Tell us." Father's head is an outline against the strong sun pouring in through the windows.

"No," I say, stifling a sob. "I'm just confused. Where's Jessie?"

"Jessie's at home, she called us from the hospital," Mom says. "She said someone hit you on the head with a bottle."

I remember screams. I remember Marsha Randall, Tomper, Jessie. I don't remember a bottle.

I am slowly becoming aware of an itchy, crusty material on my face and bits of string trailing on my cheeks. I raise my hands to my face, but Mom stops me.

"Your face was cut, Ellen," she says. "Those are stitches. Don't touch them."

For a minute, all three of us just look at each other. Father clears his throat. "Your friend — Tom is his name? — was very helpful," he says, turning away slightly and rubbing his eyes under his glasses. "He used his shirt as a compress on your face before you got to the hospital."

"As a compress?" I almost shout. "What does my face look like?"

Father hands me a small pocket mirror that he always keeps in his white coat. I gag when I see myself. I have three jagged lines running down my face and numerous little nicks. The large lines are held together by what looks like brown fishing line, and the stitching is messy and uneven; even Frankenstein's monster had neater stitches.

Clots of crusted blood the color of instant coffee cling to my face.

"I have to go to school in two weeks," I whisper. "My face is ruined."

Mom pats my shoulder with thin fingers. "We'll talk about school later," she says.

There is a clomping noise of a bunch of feet in the hall. In walks Tomper, Jessie, Mike, and Beth.

"Hi Dr. and Mrs. Sung," Jessie says. "Hope we're not interrupting."

"No, no," Father says, pushing his glasses up on his nose. "I have to make my rounds now anyway."

"I'll be back this afternoon," Mom says. "You'll be having some x-rays, and then your father and I will take you home."

"The minute my parents leave, Jessie falls on my bed, hugging me. "Jesus," she says. "I'm so glad to see you, Ellen. I didn't sleep a wink. For a minute last night, I thought you were dead."

"How're you feeling?" Tomper says, patting me on the shoulder. It's only now that I realize I'm wearing one of those ridiculous backless hospital gowns.

"You're a contender," Mike says. "You gave Marsha a major crack in the jaw."

"Ugh," I groan. "I don't want to talk about that."

"I brought you some reading," Beth says quickly, handing me a copy of *Love Story*. Ryan O'Neal and Ali MacGraw's faces smile brightly out at us. "It's set at Harvard," she says.

"Thanks, Beth," I say.

An uneasy silence settles on us like dust. Tomper fixes the blinds so the sun doesn't hit me as hard. I try to think of something funny to say, but I can't.

Still, when everyone gets ready to leave, I am almost unbearably sad to see them go.

"I'll call you at home tonight," Jessie says, squeezing my arm.

As soon as the door shuts behind them, I feel like crying, but the tears won't come. I reach for *Love Story*.

ℒ Twenty=two

"THE POLICE WANT TO talk to you," Mom tells me, just days after I've returned home.

"I don't want to go, Mom," I say. She is in my room watching me fill up a box — my third.

I start stuffing the box with books off my shelf. "I just want to forget about it."

"I know you do," Mom says. "But they can't punish that girl until they have your side of the story."

"But I feel so ugly with my dumb stitches," I say.

Mom reaches over and puts her hand on my head.

"Maybe this will help you heal, Myong-Ok," she says. "From the inside."

Mom drives me to the police station, where I have to sit alone with an officer.

"Hello," the man says. He is a big blue whale in his uniform. He takes his police hat off. "My name is Al Griffith. Can I get you a pop, some water — anything?"

"No, thanks," I say, sitting up in the chair. "I'm ready."

"All right," he says, taking up a clipboard. "Please tell

me what occurred between you and Marsha Jean Randall on the night of August 18."

I tell him about her calling me names. I remember each name exactly. I tell him about the fight — including my hitting her in the jaw — and I tell him that I don't remember the bottle incident, but my friends do.

He wants me to name my friends, so I do, one by one.

"That's good, Ellen," he says. "Now, do you want to press charges?"

"Press charges?" I say. "What will happen to Marsha?"

"Well, there are several counts you could press against her — reckless endangerment or assault, for example. If these charges hold, she could possibly spend some time in jail."

I try to picture Marsha behind bars. After all this, I realize, I don't hate her, I just feel strangely depressed: I think I can speak for myself now, but that doesn't mean that racist people are going to go away. There will probably always be people like Marsha or Brad who won't like me, without ever knowing who exactly I am.

"No charges," I say, in a voice I can barely hear.

Mr. Griffith looks up at me, surprised. "You're sure, now. It looks like that young lady did you some serious injury."

I carefully touch a fingertip to one of my cuts — it still really hurts.

"No charges," I say, then sigh. "It's not going to change things."

*

The next week, my stitches come off. My cuts are bubble-gum pink and puffy, like long worms trailing down my face. Some of the smaller nicks have scabbed.

"Ellen," Mom says, as she sees me dumping more stuff into another suitcase, "are you actually thinking of going next week?"

"Yes," I say, carefully packing my Sid the Killer T-shirts.

"Your father and I thought it might be better to wait until the next semester."

"No," I say. "By next semester everyone will have made their friends. Besides, I'm not sick. I can go now."

"But your face —"

I feel a sinking in the pit of my stomach.

"People are just going to have to take me as I am," I say.

Mom looks at me. "You are making your own decisions now," she says.

I can hear a little grace note of pride in her voice.

*

Two days before I leave, Tomper and I say goodbye. We drive out to the Sand Pits, which is deserted. In the car, we are like peas in a pod under a huge sky.

"Do you remember that party out here last fall?" I say.

Tomper looks at me and grins. "How could I forget? I remember thinking, that one, Ellen, is special."

We wrap our arms around each other and kiss, the way we did that first time under the rustling pines.

Maybe Beth is right, that when we're thirty, high school will seem like an absurdly short time, but right now I am here and warm with Tomper, and I don't want to let him go.

"I'm so sad, El," he says, and I see a tear roll down his cheek just before he buries his face in my hair. "I'm just getting to really know you, and now we have to break up."

I put my arms around him. I have never seen a boy cry before. Never.

"Please don't cry," I say, feeling my own tears starting to rise.

As we hold each other, I feel just a little bit better knowing that wherever I go, I will still have him and Jessie and Arkin stuck in my heart, like a tattoo.

*

I save my last night for Jessie. We try to draw the night out: first we go to dinner, then we sit around in my room, feeling miserable. We don't even talk. We just sit there and watch the dumb clock — a portable alarm clock I borrowed from Mom.

Finally, the clock's hands drag to midnight, and both of us are getting drowsy. Jessie gathers her stuff.

Outside, by her car, we hug for a long time.

"I'm sure going to miss you," she says, gulping for air like a fish. "You'd better write — or else."

"Let's stay best friends, okay?" I say, feeling my voice grow thin, tightwire-taut.

Jessie looks so small in the night. She digs out an envelope from her pocket and pushes it toward me.

"Here, something for you," she mumbles. "Don't read it till I'm gone."

She leaps into her car and drives into the night.

Back in my room, I open the envelope to find a poem:

We've been friends through the years,
Seen the laughter, seen the tears,
But though I've seen the sun rise and set,
There hasn't been a single soul yet,
To be a friend more true and true,
For me, it'll always be you.

I read it again, then slip it carefully into my suitcase before my vision blurs too much.

🦢 Twenty=three

T HE NEXT DAY, we all drive out to the Hibbing airport. There, a tiny shuttle plane will bring me and all my stuff to Minneapolis, where I'll take a Northwest flight to Boston's Logan Airport.

Jessie, Beth, Tomper, and Mike have all come to say goodbye to me. I'm scared, though. How am I going to say goodbye to Mom and Father and all my friends without breaking down and bawling?

I glance out the airport windows and see the needle-nosed plane fly in.

"Nice crop duster," Mike says of the small and skinny propeller plane. Twelve passengers will sit in the tiny plane, which looks like a cross between a mosquito and a minnow.

The man who was out on the runway guiding the plane in helps gas it up, then reenters the building to collect tickets.

Father slips me some bills, neatly folded.

"You and your sister have a pleasant dinner," he says.

Michelle nicely agreed to meet me at the airport to help me carry my stuff back to Cambridge.

"Thanks, Father," I say, my eyes misting already. I hug him and Mom at the same time.

Then I hug Tomper.

He kisses me on the mouth — in front of my parents! — and grins. Mike cheers.

Then I hug Beth, then Mike, each for a long time. I save Jessie for last.

"Thanks for the poem. I loved it," I whisper into her ear. "Thanks for everything."

Jessie's eyes are red around the rims, and I see her swallow and try to smile.

I grab my stuff and walk out into the bright sunlight. When I'm out on the tarmac, I look up at the sky and thank God for my family, my friends. After all that's happened to me this year, the pain was worth it.

I sit in my seat, and I wave. The propellers start; first I hear the one on the other side, and then the one on my side turns into a blur. With its mosquito drone, the plane bumbles down the runway, then bounces up, tilting into the waiting sky. I keep waving and waving like an idiot, as if I'm waiting for my hand to fall off.

The airplane rises higher and higher, yet I wave. If I look closely, I can almost imagine Mom, Father, and all my friends waving from the tiny airport below.